Breaking & Entering

BECKY RAINBIRD

Illustrated by Katie Wood

EGMONT

Special thanks to:
Victoria Connelly, West Jesmond Primary School, Maney
Hill Primary School and Courthouse Junior School

EGMONT
We bring stories to life

Breaking and Entering first published in Great Britain 2008
by Egmont UK Limited
239 Kensington High Street, London W8 6SA

Text & illustration © 2008 Egmont UK Ltd
Text by Victoria Connelly
Illustrations by Katie Wood

ISBN 978 1 4052 3943 1

1 3 5 7 9 10 8 6 4 2

A CIP catalogue record for this title is available
from the British Library

Typeset by Avon DataSet Ltd, Bidford on Avon, Warwickshire
Printed and bound in Great Britain by the CPI Group

LAURIE

NAME: Laurie Hunt

AGE: 14

NATIONALITY: British

STUDYING: Singing, drama

ROLE IN LUCKY SIX:
Lead singer and songwriter

PERSONALITY: Inquisitive

INSTANT-MESSAGE NAME: LuckyStar

JACK

NAME: Jack Hunt

AGE: 12

NATIONALITY: British

STUDYING: Music

ROLE IN LUCKY SIX:
Bass guitarist

PERSONALITY: Cheeky

INSTANT-MESSAGE NAME: CaptainJack

AIMI

NAME: Aimi Akita

AGE: 13

NATIONALITY: Japanese

STUDYING: Music

ROLE IN LUCKY SIX:
Lead guitarist and wannabe singer/songwriter

PERSONALITY: Outspoken

INSTANT-MESSAGE NAME: RockChick

MARYBETH

NAME: Marybeth Fellows

AGE: 13

NATIONALITY: American

STUDYING: Music, dance

ROLE IN LUCKY SIX:
Keyboard player

PERSONALITY: Caring

INSTANT-MESSAGE NAME: CurlyGirly

ELLE

NAME: Elle Beaumont

AGE: 14

NATIONALITY: French

STUDYING: Singing, dance

ROLE IN LUCKY SIX:
Band manager and backing singer

PERSONALITY: Very efficient!

INSTANT-MESSAGE NAME: ElleB

NOAH

NAME: Noah Hansen

AGE: 14

NATIONALITY: American

STUDYING: Music, drama

ROLE IN LUCKY SIX:
Drummer

PERSONALITY: Laid back

INSTANT-MESSAGE NAME: DrummerDude

SASHA

NAME: Sasha Quinn-Jones

AGE: 13

NATIONALITY: British

STUDYING: Dance

PERSONALITY:
A snooty show-off who's got it in for Lucky Six

CHELSEA

NAME: Chelsea Woods

AGE: 13

NATIONALITY: British

STUDYING: Dance

PERSONALITY:
Sasha's sidekick – with more talent in her little finger than her friend has in her entire body . . .

Chapter One

When you think about it, if I hadn't had the row with Aimi – the bigger than normal, pretty much enormous row – none of this might have happened. The two of us argue all the time. She's one of my best friends, and a brilliant guitarist, but she's got this thing about being the centre of attention. Mostly, our rows flare up, one of us storms off and then we're back to normal after a few hours. This time, though, Aims turned up at every rehearsal in a stinking mood. We were meant to be rehearsing for a gig Elle had booked at the shopping mall in our local town centre, and I'd written out a list of songs I thought we should play.

'Why is it always you who gets to decide, Laurie?' snapped Aimi, as I passed it round.

1

'Er, maybe because I was the one who spent all of last night going through our songs instead of watching lame-brain TV,' I said.

'Who even says we need a list?' she argued.

'OK,' I said, 'we'll just rehearse everything we know, then play what we feel like on the day.'

'What's wrong with that?' she shrugged.

'Duh! It would take, like, a month, and we've got less than a week till the show.'

'Don't "duh" me,' said Aimi, raising her voice.

'Duh, I think I just did.'

I know. Mature, huh? But she was seriously getting on my nerves, *and* wasting rehearsal time.

'I've had enough of this,' she said, yanking off her guitar.

'What?'

'Following orders. Being in your stupid band,' she yelled.

'Get over yourself,' I shouted back. 'That's not how it is, and you know it.'

'Yeah?' she said. 'You know what else I know? I'm leaving. Permanently.'

2

And before anyone could stop her she snatched up her guitar case and walked out, slamming the door behind her.

None of us believed it for a second – Aimi's all about playing the drama queen. For once, though, we were wrong. Three days later, we'd all tried changing her mind, but it seemed like a total lost cause.

'She *can't* leave,' said Marybeth. 'I mean, I know she can be a pain, but things wouldn't be the same without her.'

We were sitting in the common room, Marybeth, Elle, Jack, Noah and me. Sort of an emergency meeting to work out what we were going to do.

'Maybe we should set up auditions,' said Jack. 'You know, in case she definitely does leave.'

He is so sensitive.

'I thought you liked Aimi,' said Elle.

'I do,' Jack told her. 'I'm just saying.'

'Well, don't,' I snapped.

'Just because she won't listen to you,' said Jack. 'I nearly had her convinced yesterday. She was seriously thinking about changing her mind.'

I looked at him doubtfully.

'It's true,' said Marybeth. 'We both went to see her, but she didn't want to back down.'

'You heard about her parents?' said Noah.

I shook my head.

'About them cancelling their visit?' said Marybeth, and Noah nodded. 'They called at the weekend and told her they had to stay in Tokyo because they're working on this really important project.'

4

Something clicked into place in my brain.

'*That's* why she was in such a foul mood at the rehearsal,' I said.

'I guess,' said Marybeth. 'You know how much she'd been looking forward to seeing them.'

'I wish she'd hurry up and get over it,' said Jack. 'We're going to sound rubbish on Saturday without her.'

Elle shook her head. 'I asked her about that. She's still leaving, but she says she hasn't left yet, so she'll play on Saturday.'

'No way!' said Marybeth.

'How did you persuade her?' I asked.

'It wasn't easy,' said Elle, 'and she's not exactly thrilled about it, but I told her she'd agreed to the booking months ago, before she decided to leave, and it would be unprofessional not to be there.'

'Cunning,' said Noah admiringly.

'I told you she didn't really want to go,' said Jack, leaning back in his chair and swinging his feet up on to the table.

But I had a feeling it would take more than a few

5

hours at Lowfield Shopping Centre to change Aimi's
mind.

By the time Saturday morning arrived, despite what
Elle had said, I was still half expecting Aimi to bail
out at the last minute. So I was seriously relieved
when I saw her trudging down the front steps of the
academy to meet us.

'All set?' said Miss Diamond, our singing teacher
and chaperone for the gig.

I nodded, and we piled into the school minibus
(which doubles as our very glamorous tour bus) as
she started the engine.

It felt strange, the six of us being together again, as
if it had been longer than a week since my row with
Aimi. Part of me had been hoping Jack was right, that
playing the gig together would convince Aimi to stay,
but as we arrived and set up in a strained kind of
silence, it began to seem less and less likely.

'Hey,' said Noah, peering out over the makeshift

stage into the gathering crowd, 'who d'you reckon that guy is?'

I followed the direction of his gaze and saw a short, balding man wearing a badly fitting pinstripe suit, purple braces and a cowboy hat.

'No idea,' I said. 'Maybe he's finally woken up to the fact his wardrobe is a disaster and he's here for the shopping.'

Noah grinned.

'Looks like a talent scout to me,' said Elle, coming up behind us.

'You think?' I said.

'Yep. You can tell by the outfit.'

I checked my watch. 'Five minutes,' I said. 'I guess we'd better hurry up if we want to impress him.'

Considering the weird atmosphere in the minibus, and the fact we hadn't rehearsed with Aimi in over a week, the gig went pretty well. The small crowd who'd gathered at the start had grown to more or less fill the mall by the time we finished.

'Thank you, Lowfield, and goodnight!' shouted Jack into my microphone as we made our way offstage.

'Cut the cheese, Wart-face,' I hissed, dragging him away. 'There's a talent scout in the audience and I don't want him thinking we're all losers.'

I scrambled down off the back of the stage, following the others, and ducked into the curtained backstage area.

'A talent scout?' said Jack, catching up with me a minute later. 'Where?'

I pulled a bottle of water out of my bag and took a swig.

'I don't know,' I said. 'Somewhere out in the crowd.'

'Try over there,' said Elle, pointing through a gap in the back of the curtains. 'He grabbed Aimi the second she stepped offstage.'

'Why would he only want to talk to her?'

'Maybe she's telling him about all of us. You know, kind of as a representative of the band,' said Noah.

'The band she's about to leave,' said Elle doubtfully.

'He looks a bit dodgy to me,' said Jack.

He had a point.

'I think we should go over there,' I said decisively. 'She's not exactly safe, hanging about talking to a total stranger.'

Elle nodded. 'Come on,' she said, and we made our way across to Aimi and the talent scout.

'Nice to meet you, ladies,' he said, once we'd introduced ourselves. Aimi scowled. 'Rich Saunders,' the talent scout added, fishing two business cards out of his pocket and handing one to each of us. Elle looked down at hers and frowned.

'That was quite a performance back there,' he said. 'Not a bad little band you've got going.'

'Thanks,' I said uncertainly.

'This little lady's your star, of course,' he continued. 'Very talented guitarist. I was just telling her how keen I am to hear more of her stuff. Solo material, that is,' he added, just in case we got the wrong end of the stick.

9

'Really?' I said, looking straight at Aimi and raising my eyebrows.

'Really,' she said, and to prove her point she pulled a CD out of her bag and handed it to Mr Saunders.

'It's got all my solo stuff on it.' She pointed to the track listing, just beneath her name, a photo of herself and our web address. 'Like I was saying, I don't just play guitar. I write songs, and sing too. I've never really had the chance to do either in the band,' she said pointedly. 'That's why I want to go solo.'

'Lovely,' said Mr Saunders, dropping the CD into his pocket. 'I'll have a listen, and you give me a call in a few days, when you've had time to think things over. You've got my card.'

He reached out and shook her hand, then walked off into the crowd of shoppers.

Elle and I took all of two seconds to drag Aimi backstage again.

'What on earth was that about?' I hissed.

Aimi laughed. 'Someone's finally recognised I'm more talented than you are. Get over it.'

'I don't even think he's a real talent scout,' said Elle, who's way better at ignoring Aimi's insults than I am. 'His record label,' she said, flapping the business card under Aimi's nose, 'I've never heard of them.'

'What, and you know *all* the record labels, do you?' snapped Aimi. 'You just can't handle the fact he wants me and not you.'

And before either of us had a chance to argue she stalked off towards the exit.

If things in the minibus had been uncomfortable on the way to the gig, they were a million times worse as we drove back to school.

'Is anything wrong?' asked Miss Diamond.

You'd pretty much have had to be a lump of rock with no eyes, no ears and no brains, not to realise something was going on.

'I'm fine,' said Aimi. 'I just out-performed everyone today and some people can't handle it.'

Miss Diamond didn't seem to know what to say and, not daring to start another argument in front of her, the minibus fell into miserable silence again.

I sat there, wondering for the millionth time that week what it would be like playing without Aimi. It wasn't as if the band would fall apart without her – when our bass player left last year, splitting up didn't occur to any of us – but we wouldn't find another guitarist at the academy as good. Maybe there were more important things than being the best, though. Things like chilling out instead of flying off the handle all the time. I glanced over at Aimi again. She glared back at me and, however hard I tried to stop it, one thought kept creeping into my head – would it be such a bad thing if she did leave?

Chapter Two

That night, I tried going to see Aimi loads of times, but she was always on her phone, nattering away in Japanese. I guess there's no good translation for the English 'wow!' cos I heard it a lot. Aimi could only have been talking to her parents, probably about the new project delaying their visit – another totally cool gadget we'd all be desperate to get ourselves.

I got a watery smile the next day, which is often as close to 'sorry' as Aimi gets and, as the weeks went by, luckily for the band, she seemed to relax back into her old self.

It was really strange that Aimi didn't hear anything from the talent scout – she seemed so sure that she would. So, one day, we all found ourselves huddled over a computer doing a search for the music label on the guy's business card.

'Are you sure you've typed in the name right?' Aimi said, hovering over my left shoulder.

'Of course I'm sure,' I groaned. 'Look! Nothing's coming up. *You* try.' We swapped places at the computer and Aimi typed the music label – Slick Riff Records – into the search engine. Marybeth, Noah, Jack, Elle and I watched as Aimi clicked on page after page.

'Is that it?' Noah asked.

'No, silly,' Marybeth said. 'That's a pizza company.'

Noah groaned while Jack did his best to suppress his giggles.

We stared at the computer, our faces glowing in its light, as we scanned page after page in the hope of finding something.

'Oh, this is useless!' Aimi moaned a couple of minutes later. 'Maybe he gave me the wrong card.'

I glared at her. As much as I didn't want to upset her, somebody had to tell her the truth. 'If you ask me, it all sounds a bit dodgy,' I said. 'I wouldn't trust him, Aims. He could be anyone.'

She pouted.

'Laurie's right,' Marybeth said. 'It's probably some kind of weird scam.'

Aimi sighed. I could see that she was disappointed and I felt really bad for her. Mrs Walsh, our classical dance teacher here at the academy, is always telling us how difficult it is to make it in the entertainment industry because there's so much competition, and Aimi had really thought that this might've been her lucky break. I watched as she picked up the business card from the desk and put it in her pocket.

I bit my lip. 'You're not going to try to ring him, are you?' I asked her.

She looked up at me and, for a moment, I thought she was about to sneak off with her mobile and make the call. 'No,' she said finally. 'I think you're right.'

'You don't need him anyway,' Noah said.

'Yeah,' Jack agreed. 'You've got us.'

We all smiled at Aimi.

'Lucky Six wouldn't be lucky without you,' I said.

'And it wouldn't be six either,' Elle pointed out.

We all laughed and Aimi seemed a little bit happier.

I put my hand on her shoulder and gave her a squeeze. 'And *I've* got a brilliant idea.'

'What?' everyone said.

'We could play one of Aimi's songs at the battle-of-the-bands competition.'

'Excellent!' Noah said, his blue eyes twinkling with enthusiasm.

'It might even be a good time to have her doing

some more singing,' I continued, aware that Aimi totally loves praise.

'Yeah,' Elle said. 'You've got a great voice, Aimi.'

I tried not to flinch at Elle's admiration. Elle's such a perfectionist so praise from her really counts. I bit my lip and tried my best to keep smiling. I have to admit that there's always been a bit of friendly rivalry between Aimi and me. We both enjoy being the centre of attention and we're both really ambitious too. I couldn't help feeling a little left out as Elle praised Aimi.

Aimi grinned. 'I know,' she said. 'I guess my voice is pretty good.' And then she laughed.

Things, it seemed, were back to normal again. What a relief!

So, when Aimi didn't show up for our next rehearsal, we were all a bit surprised.

'Maybe she's changed her mind again,' Noah said, from his home behind the drums.

'Do you think she went and rang that man after all?' Elle said, neatly tucking a strand of glossy brown hair behind her ear.

I shook my head. 'She said she wouldn't.'

'But you saw how disappointed she was, Laurie,' Elle said. 'I wouldn't be surprised if she's signing a contract right now.'

Marybeth sighed from behind the keyboards. 'We were meant to be playing one of her songs today. Surely she wouldn't miss that.'

'I know,' I said.

'And if she is going to leave us, she needs to do it officially and give proper notice,' Elle said – ever the manager.

Just then my younger brother Jack turned up, carrying his bass guitar. I must admit that I was none too happy when Jack joined Lucky Six. I'd always thought of it as *my* band and I really didn't like the idea of my little brother muscling in, but the others thought he was great, and I had to admit that he was a really talented musician.

'Late as usual, Wart-face,' I said. He ignored me. 'Did you see Aimi on your way over?' I asked, knowing that he'd been back to the dorms to get his guitar before coming to join us.

'No. Isn't she here?' he asked, ruffling his messy red hair and looking around. He really was a hopeless case.

'If she was here, I wouldn't be asking you if you'd seen her, you dope.' I shook my head.

'All right, keep your hair on, sis,' Jack said.

'She was meant to be here ten minutes ago,' I said.

'Where do you think she is?' Marybeth asked.

'She's probably decided to go solo again,' Noah said.

'Don't say that,' I told him, but I was getting a bit worried. 'I'm going over to her dorm.'

As I walked back to the girls' dorms, I was thinking about how annoyed I was by Aimi's behaviour – after all the support we'd given her, she could've at least turned up on time – but there was a part of me that was anxious for her too. What if she'd done something stupid like gone behind our backs and called that dodgy man?

Reaching the girls' dorms, I went straight to Aimi's room and knocked on her door but there was no response.

'Aimi?' I called. 'Are you in there?' I knocked again and then decided to open the door and peep inside. The dorm doors are never locked – it's against the rules.

'Aimi?' The room was empty and Aimi was nowhere to be seen but that wasn't the reason why I gasped. The room was a complete mess and I mean *mess*. I've seen some untidy rooms in my time – after all, I do have two brothers and I've seen the chaos that is Noah's – but Aimi's was in a right state and I was beginning to get seriously worried. Drawers had been left open and their contents spilled all over the floor. Her wardrobe door was open and there were clothes everywhere. Her bed had been moved and the pillows – like everything else – were on the floor. Who could have done such a thing? Surely not Aimi? She could be a bit impatient at times and had been known to throw the odd strop, but she wouldn't have completely wrecked her own room, would she?

Backing out, I shut the door slowly behind me, then found my mobile and rang Aimi's number.

Where was she? I got my answer when I heard her footsteps from down the corridor and heard her mobile ringing.

'Hello?' Aimi's voice said. It sounded really wobbly and I heard it in stereo because it was then that she appeared from round the corner clutching a handful of loo roll. She'd obviously been in the girls' toilets.

'Aimi?' I said, switching my phone off as I saw her. Aimi hung up too. 'What's the matter?' I asked,

noticing that her eyes were all red and watery. Poor Aimi, I thought. She'd been crying.

'Laurie,' she began, her voice sounding very distant, 'I don't know what's going on. I got back to my room after class to get my guitar and lyrics book for rehearsal and I just –'

'What?' I asked.

'My room,' she said. 'It's completely wrecked!'

'No kidding. Has anything been taken?' I asked. She flung the door open and we stared at the upheaval in silence.

Aimi shrugged. 'I'm not sure.'

Suddenly, she was crying again and I felt really bad for having all those mean thoughts before, about her not turning up to the rehearsal. I should've known it wasn't like Aimi to let us down.

'Don't worry, Aims,' I said, putting my arm round her. 'We'll work out what's going on. Don't forget, Lucky Six are pretty good when it comes to solving mysteries.'

Aimi blew her nose and shook her head vehemently. Out of the six of us, she was the least

23

keen on getting involved in solving mysteries, but I can't help always wanting to get to the bottom of things. Perhaps that's what comes of having parents who work for the police force. I seem to have a nose for trouble, and I can't think of anything more exciting than cracking a case – other than singing with our fabulous band, of course.

I found a clean tissue in my pocket and Aimi blew her nose again and mopped her eyes. It was a shock seeing her cry; she was normally so confident and sure of herself. I felt my blood boil that somebody could do something this nasty to my friend.

'Come on,' I said. 'We've got to find Mrs Walsh or Ms Lang right away and tell them what's happened.'

Chapter Three

Mrs Walsh was tidying up one of the dance studios when we found her but she stopped what she was doing when she heard what had happened, marching across the campus back to the girls' dorm with us.

'This is just terrible!' she blurted, walking into Aimi's room and surveying the mess. 'Is anything missing?'

For a moment, I thought Aimi was going to cry again like she had when I'd asked her the exact same question.

'I'm not sure,' Aimi said, shrugging hopelessly. 'I don't think so.'

'You'll have to check very carefully,' Mrs Walsh said. 'We want to be absolutely sure what we're dealing with here.' She shook her head. 'I can't understand it. Who could've done such a thing?'

We all looked around the room again as if searching for clues.

'We'll have to tell Ms Lang,' Mrs Walsh announced. 'She's not going to be happy about this, I can tell you.'

Sure enough, Ms Lang was informed about the break-in and made an announcement in assembly the very next morning.

'This kind of behaviour will *not* be tolerated at The Verity Lang Academy.' Her hazel eyes – normally filled with kindness – glared out at the entire school.

'Blimey, I've never seen her so angry,' I whispered to Elle, who was sitting beside me.

'We need to get to the bottom of this,' Ms Lang continued, 'and quickly too. If anybody here knows anything at all about this appalling break-in, then

they should come to my office immediately after assembly.'

A horrible silence fell over the assembly hall. Nobody dared to move but everyone's eyes glanced left and right, wondering if anyone had any information at all.

'She'll set Mister Binks on anyone who dares to confess,' Elle whispered to me. I nudged her in the ribs and tried not to burst out laughing at the idea of Ms Lang's little white poodle snapping at the guilty party.

Still, silence.

'Very well,' Ms Lang said, looking down at her pupils with disappointment. 'We shall see.'

Over the next few days, we couldn't stop talking about Aimi and the break-in – whenever she wasn't about, of course. We didn't want to keep upsetting her so we kept our ideas to ourselves until we were alone.

'What do you think the school's going to do about it?' Elle asked. She's always been a stickler for things being done the right way.

'But we don't know if anything's been stolen yet,' I pointed out.

'Then why would someone have broken in like that?' Noah asked.

I shrugged. 'I don't know.'

'It's got to be an inside job,' Jack said, sounding as if he'd been watching one too many cop films or listening to our parents and the way they spoke about cases.

'What makes you think that? It could've been anyone,' I said. 'I don't think it's that hard to get on campus and the rooms in the dorms aren't locked, are they?'

Jack sighed and we were all silent for a moment.

'Why do you think it was someone from the school, Jack?' Marybeth asked.

He frowned, his freckly forehead wrinkling. 'What if it's someone trying to scare Aimi away?'

'Why would someone do that?' Noah asked.

'Maybe they've heard she's thinking of going solo and they want to take her place in Lucky Six. Scaring her enough to leave the academy might just do the trick. I can think of hundreds of really good guitarists who would do anything to take her place.'

I glared at him. 'Really?' I said sarcastically.

'Well, half a dozen at least,' Jack said.

It was my turn to frown. 'I don't know.'

'Do you still think she wants to leave the band?' Elle asked, her pretty face anxious.

'She's not talked about it since we did that computer search for Rich Saunders' non-existent music label,' I said.

'Doesn't mean she isn't thinking about it, though, does it?' Jack said.

We all stared at each other. No one looked happy. We were such a great team. For a moment, I thought back over all the brilliant times we'd had together – the rehearsals, the songwriting, gigs – and I couldn't bear to think of us not all being together.

'I don't get it,' Marybeth said.

'What?' Jack said.

'Aimi's having way more than her share of bad luck all at once. Her parents having to stay away to work so hard. That weird guy from the record company. The break-in.'

I sneezed. My nose was itching like mad.

Noah nodded. 'I know how she feels,' he said, nodding his head. 'It's like that time last week when I got out of bed and stubbed my big toe and banged my head at the same time.'

Elle sighed. 'It's not like that at all, Noah! This is much more serious. Still, it's possible that all this *is* just bad luck. But I'm still worried she'll decide to leave the band.'

Things pretty much got back to normal after that for a while. We went to classes: classical dance with Mrs Walsh who always works us really hard; modern dance with Mr Martinez who likes to wear really wacky outfits in his attempt to encourage 'freedom of expression' as he always says; and drama classes with Mrs D'Silva who was really famous in the 1970s and totally believes that Elle will make it big one day. And, at every opportunity, we got together to rehearse for the battle-of-the-bands competition.

It was at the end of a particularly good session one evening – when Aimi had shown off her skills as a singer to one of her own songs – that she told us she'd phoned her parents.

'Did you tell them about the break-in?' Marybeth asked.

'Of course. That's why I rang them, although I was really dreading it in case they said I had to leave the school and come home. They're not too keen on me being here as it is.'

'Why not?' Noah asked.

'I think they'd rather have me in some boring old music academy, permanently attached to my violin,' Aimi said, rolling her eyes.

It was true – Aimi was a totally brilliant violinist and her parents were so proud of her. They couldn't understand that she wanted more than just to develop her classical talent.

'So what did they say?' Noah asked, fiddling anxiously with his lucky drumsticks.

'They were really worried, but they wanted to thank you, Laurie, for reporting it to Mrs Walsh. They said they trusted that Ms Lang would get to the bottom of it and hope that whoever trashed my room is caught soon.'

'Absolutely,' Elle said, shivering theatrically. 'I

hate to think of someone wandering around out there. I mean, it could happen again, couldn't it?'

'Don't!' Marybeth said. 'It gives me the creeps.'

'I'm sure everything'll be sorted soon,' Noah said, throwing up a drumstick and catching it with casual ease. I grinned at him and he smiled back. I instantly felt myself blushing.

'Yes,' I said. 'If Ms Lang and Mister Binks are on the case.'

We all laughed and Jack did a yappy impression of Mister Binks's high-pitched bark.

'That's not all,' Aimi said suddenly.

We all stopped laughing – and barking – wondering what she was going to say.

'My parents had a break-in too.'

'*What?*' I said. 'When?'

'A few weeks ago. Just before we played at Lowfield Shopping Centre. Someone broke into their office.'

'And did they take anything?' Jack asked.

'No,' Aimi said, shaking her head, her blue streaks catching the light. 'But Mum and Dad think they know what they were after.'

We all leaned forward slightly.

'They've been working on a brand-new gadget.'

'Cool!' Noah and Jack said together. They're gadget crazy and always love hearing about Aimi's parents' latest inventions.

'I knew it!' I said. 'What are they working on? Are we allowed to know?'

Aimi looked thrilled to be the centre of attention. She's as proud of her parents as they are

of her and she loves talking about their new gadgets. She cleared her throat, as if she were going to sing about their latest one to us.

'Come on, Aimi,' I said. 'Get on with it.'

'All right, all right. Just cos you're jealous cos *your* parents don't invent cool things,' Aimi said.

'No,' I said, blushing at how close to the truth it was. 'Our parents just arrest people who steal them.'

'Anyway,' Aimi continued, 'before I was so rudely interrupted, I was going to tell you about this really amazing new gadget. It's called a jukebox watch. It plays music, videos – everything.'

We all stared at her, our mouths open and our eyes wide with wonder. Even I had to admit that it sounded pretty awesome.

'Wow!' Noah said. 'That sounds mega.'

'And the really cool thing is it's totally waterproof so you can even swim with it on,' Aimi continued.

'So, when can you get one for us?' Jack asked.

'I doubt they'll be handing them out to me,' Aimi said. 'Security has really been stepped up since the break-in. Dad's locked the gadget away in a safe now. Only my parents and I know the combination,' Aimi added smugly.

'You know the combination?' Elle said.

'They told you?' I said.

'Of course. It was actually my idea,' Aimi said. 'It's the –' She stopped and looked around the rehearsal room as if somebody might be hiding in the shadows. We all huddled closer to listen to her. 'It's the last six digits of my mobile number,' she whispered.

I flinched. I couldn't help it. And another thing happened too – my nose started to tickle slightly again. The last time I'd had such a spell of itchy nostrils, trouble had been just around the corner. I rubbed it impatiently.

'Hey, that's really great,' Noah said, but I wasn't so sure. Mobile numbers were so easy to get hold of, weren't they? And, with the recent ransacking of Aimi's room . . . well, you couldn't be too careful who might get hold of your private information.

'Don't you think it's weird that your parents had a break-in too?' I said.

'Yeah, it's strange,' Aimi said, but she didn't seem so worried about it.

'No, I mean – don't you think it's more than a coincidence?'

'What do you mean?' Aimi asked.

'I'm not sure,' I said, suddenly feeling rather useless because I couldn't see how everything could be linked.

'Yeah, but the two break-ins happened on opposite sides of the globe, Laurie,' Noah pointed out, rolling his eyes at me. I blushed.

'Yes,' Elle agreed. 'It's just some weird coincidence.'

'Just bad luck,' Marybeth said.

'*Very* bad luck,' Elle added.

'You're reading stuff into the situation, Laurie,' Marybeth said. 'The detective in you is getting carried away – as usual!'

'Yeah!' Jack agreed. 'Inspector Laurie wants to whip the handcuffs out when there's probably some simple explanation for everything.'

'Like what, Pea-brain?' I asked, really wanting to know, but the others had lost interest in my theory and were talking about band stuff again. I sighed and sat down on a stool, going over the facts again. Two break-ins: Aimi's room and Aimi's parents'. A stranger suddenly interested in Aimi. A new gadget – the sort of gadget criminals might well want to get their hands on.

But it was no use. I really couldn't make any sense of it and it was totally doing my head in. But one thing was for certain – if the others weren't taking things seriously, then that meant I had to. They might not want to solve this mystery but *I* certainly did.

Chapter Four

As we flung ourselves into another rehearsal for the battle-of-the-bands competition, I couldn't help thinking how lucky we were. I sang one of my very own songs at the front of the stage and looked around me. There was Elle – the best backing singer in the school and our much-loved manager, her stylish brown bob swinging in time to the music; sweet Marybeth on keyboards, her violet eyes shining with enthusiasm and her blonde curls swinging madly in time to the music; Jack on the bass, his eyes narrowed in concentration and his scruffy red hair glowing under the stage lights; gorgeous Noah on the drums, his sandy-brown hair flopping adorably over his eyes; and, luckily for us, Aimi, giving it all

39

she had on her guitar like a real pro. Lucky Six, I thought. Lucky to still be together, doing the thing that we all loved best in the world: performing.

I thought about how close we'd come to losing Aimi and what a nightmare that would've been. I couldn't imagine anyone else in the school taking her place. I smiled, thinking that a little compromise went a long way and knowing that, after my song had finished, we'd be launching into one or two of Aimi's numbers to keep her happy. And I had to admit that it was really good letting Aimi have more input. So she wasn't as good a songwriter as me – I'd never admit that even if she was now, would I? But it was always great for the band to have new material.

Things were going well between the two of us, even with the friendly rivalry thing going: trying to outdo each other onstage.

'Laurie! Do you mind not *shrieking* out my lyrics? I'll sing the song myself if you insist on killing it like that.'

'Well, I can't hear myself think with you

hammering your guitar like that.'

'My guitar is just as important as your precious voice. Blimey, Laurie, you're such a primer donna.'

'*Prima* donna, idiot! Primer is some sort of paint!'

But the rivalry thing wasn't a *bad* thing. It usually got the very best performance out of us and that was surely good for the band and good for the upcoming competition too. Miss Diamond was always telling us about the importance of passion in a performance, and Aimi and I definitely had that in spades.

I'd even managed to put the break-ins out of my mind so that I could focus more on the competition. I had to admit that there were more important things to think about right now. My sleuthing skills would have to be put on hold.

A few days later, Aimi turned up to rehearsal with a frown on her face and we all thought the worst

41

– there'd been another break-in . . .

But, thankfully, Aimi shook her head. 'No,' she said, 'but I have lost something.'

'What?' we all asked.

She flopped down on the stage, her legs dangling over the edge. 'Some files have gone missing from my desktop.'

'Oh, no!' I said, knowing how annoying that can be, having lost so many of my own, like the fool I am.

Noah didn't look convinced. 'Are you *sure* they're missing?'

'What do you mean?' Aimi snapped back, obviously not liking Noah's line of questioning.

'I mean, are you sure you haven't just – you know – misplaced them?'

'Of course I haven't misplaced them! I'm not completely disorganised like *some* people,' Aimi said, giving Noah the evil eye.

'Noah's just saying!' I said, thinking Aimi's comment was a bit below the belt, even though Noah could win medals for being messy.

'Yeah,' Jack said, 'he was only trying to help.'

Aimi suddenly leaped down off the stage. 'I don't know why I bothered telling you guys. If you're not going to take me seriously, I'll just have to deal with it on my own.' And, with that, she stormed out of the music room.

'Don't be like that, Aimi,' Marybeth called.

'Aimi!' I yelled after her. The door slammed. 'And she had the nerve to call *me* the prima donna!'

'We'd better go after her and sort this out,' Elle said, and we left the boys in the music room.

'Aimi – wait,' I said, as we all caught up with her on the way back to the girls' dorms.

Aimi stopped and glared back at us. 'What?'

'You didn't really give us much of a chance back there, did you?' Elle said.

'We want to help – really,' Marybeth said.

'You know what Noah's like. It always takes a boy to put his foot in it,' I said.

Aimi gave a little smile.

'He really *did* want to help,' Elle said. 'He just didn't go about it the right way.'

'Come on,' I said, putting my arm round Aimi's shoulders, 'let's go and have a look for these missing files.'

Soon, we were all crowded round Aimi's computer. Her room was tidy now – Aimi had carefully cleaned everything before putting it away, desperately looking for a clue to who could have done such a thing.

'Which files do you think are missing?' Marybeth asked, peering closely at the screen.

Aimi sighed angrily. 'My music files,' she said. 'Songs I've been working on lately.'

I frowned, knowing how important they'd be to her. 'Oh, Aimi.'

'Songs for my –' she paused – 'for my solo album.' She looked a little embarrassed at her confession and I wondered whether being messed about by Mr Saunders had taken the wind out of her sails a bit. She'd obviously worked so hard after meeting him, only to be badly let down. It made me so angry when I thought about it.

I rubbed my nose. 'Do you think that Mr Saunders has something to do with this?'

'What do you mean?' Aimi asked, and Elle and Marybeth stared at me.

'Maybe him, or someone from his so-called music label –'

'The one we couldn't find any trace of, you

mean?' Marybeth said.

'Exactly,' I said. 'Maybe someone's hacked into your computer and taken your files.'

Elle snorted. 'Oh, Laurie, you're going all detective on us again.'

'No, I'm not,' I said. 'I'm trying to work things out logically.'

'But how on earth would someone manage to hack into Aimi's computer?' Marybeth asked.

I shrugged. 'I don't know but it can be done if you really want to do it, can't it?' I said.

'You might have a good point,' Aimi said, and I could see her eyes sparkling. I knew just what she was thinking. She was flattered by the idea that someone would go to all the trouble of hacking into her computer to steal her files. It showed she had talent and that somebody would go to any lengths to get their hands on her music.

We sat in silence for a moment, all staring at the computer and thinking. Finally, Aimi spoke.

'I think I should give him a call.'

'Who? Mr Saunders?' I said.

'No, Father Christmas,' Aimi said. *'Duh!* Of *course* Mr Saunders. I'm not sure what's going on here, but I need to find out.'

'But he probably has nothing to do with it,' Elle pointed out.

'Well, I'll soon see,' Aimi said.

I watched as Aimi found the business card that Mr Saunders had given her and got out her mobile from her jacket pocket.

'Are you sure this is a good idea?' Elle said. But

we couldn't stop Aimi. Once she had an idea in her head, it was impossible to change her mind. All we could do was huddle round the phone and listen to what was said.

We watched as Aimi punched in the number, careful to get it right, and then we waited.

Aimi hung up almost immediately.

'What happened?' Marybeth asked.

'The number's not recognised,' Aimi said, her face falling.

'Maybe he's changed it,' I said, but I didn't really believe that. First, we couldn't find his music label on the Internet and now his phone number didn't work. It was all looking extremely suspicious to me.

Aimi slammed her mobile on her desk in frustration and then she saw the business card again. Picking it up, she moved towards the keyboard once more.

'What are you doing?' I asked.

'Look,' Aimi said, 'he's got an email address. I can try that instead.'

We all watched as Aimi hastily wrote an email to Mr Saunders.

Dear Mr Saunders

I've been trying to contact you but your mobile number doesn't work. Please give me a call or send me an email so we can talk.

Regards

Aimi Akita (Lucky Six guitarist)

She took a deep breath and pressed the 'send' icon. And then we waited some more. It didn't surprise me when, seconds later, the email was returned as undeliverable.

'This is hopeless,' Elle said.

'None of his contact details is right,' I said.

'I think we should just give up. It's getting us nowhere,' Marybeth added.

Aimi sank visibly in her seat and I could see she

was seriously depressed by the whole thing and needed cheering up.

'Tell you what,' I said, 'let's check up on our web site to see if Noah's updated it.'

'Yeah, we want to make sure he's put the stuff up about the battle-of-the-bands competition,' Marybeth said.

'And got the date right,' added the super-organised Elle.

Aimi smiled. It was always fun checking out the web site. It was the home of Lucky Six on the Internet and it always gave me a thrill thinking about all the people who might be checking it out and catching up on our latest band news. We'd had such fun putting it together and there were all sorts of things on there: fab pics from our gigs, all our tour dates and a message board for our fans with loads of great comments on it.

Sure enough, Noah had done his job and put up the information about the battle of the bands. I couldn't help wondering if our fans had seen it and if they'd turn up to support us. It was a really important competition for us and I so hoped that we were going to do well – not just for us but for our loyal fans too.

'We might as well check the weblog while we're here,' I said, eager to see if there were any messages and, sure enough, there was one. But it wasn't from a fan – not exactly. It was from Mr Saunders.

I turned to look at Aimi, whose eyes had widened at the message.

'He wants my mobile number,' she said excitedly. 'He says he's got some exciting news for me and he wants to get in touch.'

Chapter Five

I swear I could feel my heart racing when I heard Aimi's words.

'I don't think you should trust him,' I said.

Aimi glared at me. She was getting very good at that lately. 'You're just jealous,' she said. 'You've always been jealous of me.'

'Yeah, right,' I retorted. 'Jealous of a stranger wanting my mobile number. And that's what he is, Aimi – a complete stranger. This could be really dangerous.'

Aimi's dark eyes narrowed in anger.

'Laurie's right,' Elle said calmly. 'Don't forget that your parents have used the last six digits of your mobile number for their combination lock.'

Marybeth nodded. 'For the gadget!'

'It would be really stupid to give it out to a virtual stranger,' Marybeth continued.

Aimi looked so angry. 'I hadn't forgotten, you know,' she said, but she cast her eyes to the floor and I couldn't help not believing her. She'd just got completely carried away by everything and you couldn't blame her really.

'And remember that we couldn't find any trace of his company on the Internet at all. I even asked my dad and he'd never heard of it either,' Elle said.

'And Elle's dad's a music mogul,' I said. 'If it was genuine, he would have heard of it.'

'He might not have!' Aimi yelled. 'He can't possibly know everyone in the whole world.'

'Aimi –' Elle began.

But Aimi wasn't listening. 'You're all just jealous. Jealous of my talent and jealous that Mr Saunders approached *me* that day and not any of you. You want to try and stop me doing well so I won't leave Lucky Six. None of you are thinking that this could be my big opportunity. You're just thinking of yourselves because you're selfish. Well, I don't want you in my room so you can all get out!'

For a moment, we all stared at her in shock. Was she serious? Aimi could throw a strop like no one else, but she'd never *ever* talked to us like that before.

I looked at Elle – her mouth was open in surprise. And Marybeth's face was as white as a ghost's.

'Go on – get out!'

We left the room hastily, jumping as Aimi slammed the door in our faces.

'Blimey! I wasn't expecting that,' I said.

'She's got a real temper on her sometimes,' Elle said.

'I think she just needs a bit of space,' Marybeth said thoughtfully.

We stood in silence for a moment.

'But what should we do now?' I whispered, aware that Aimi might hear us from the other side of the door.

'Should we tell Mrs Walsh?' Marybeth suggested.

'I don't think she'd be able to do much about it,' I said. 'They still haven't found out who broke into Aimi's room.'

'So what should we do?' Elle asked.

I sighed. It was getting pretty late now and there wasn't really much we could do, but suddenly I thought of something. 'I think we should get Noah to disable the web site ASAP.'

Elle and Marybeth nodded in agreement and I whipped my mobile phone out. We all ran to my room to make the call, narrowly avoiding Sasha and Zoe's lights-out patrol. Zoe was the year-eleven prefect and she was OK, but Sasha Quinn-Jones, the year-nine prefect, was a total witch when it came to bossing people about – especially poor Marybeth. Sasha picked on her mercilessly for being a scholarship student when her own family owned practically the whole of the UK. And I had another reason to steer clear of her too. With her long blonde hair and ice-blue eyes, she thought she was model material and, to top it all, had a crush on Noah.

'Come on,' I said over my shoulder as I led the way to my room. 'We don't want to run into Sasha.'

Finally, in the safety of my room, I rang Noah and we all explained what had happened.

'We think you should disable the site, Noah,' I said.

'Just to be safe,' Elle said.

'For a little while anyway,' Marybeth added.

'Are you *sure* you want me to do that?' Noah asked, and he sounded really anxious about it as if we didn't know what we were doing.

'Please, Noah. You've got to trust us,' I said.

'OK, Laurie,' he said softly, and my heart melted. 'I'll do it if you think it's for the best.'

I breathed a sigh of relief. We'd found a temporary solution to the problem at least.

Suddenly, there was a loud rap on the door.

'You should be in your own rooms now, girls,' Zoe's voice called. 'Time for lights out.'

'OK, Zoe, no problem,' I yelled back, glad it was her and not Sasha on the other side of my door. There was no way that I wanted Sasha getting wind of what was happening. She loved seeing things go wrong for Lucky Six and would be totally pleased to hear that we were having problems now.

'Best be off, then,' Elle said.

'Yes,' Marybeth said, 'I'm beat.'

We all looked at each other. It had been a very odd day, but we'd come through it, and we could only hope that things would get better from now on. The future of Lucky Six depended on it.

We all said goodnight and I watched Elle and Marybeth heading down the corridor to their own rooms. I closed my door, thinking of the events of the day and bit my lip. I couldn't help worrying about it all. What if we were doing everything wrong? What if this Mr Saunders was a real criminal and was out to harm Aimi in some way?

I got ready for bed, snuggling under my duvet with my mobile. I'd decided to text my mum for some advice. I didn't tell her about Mr and Mrs Akita's break-in because I couldn't fit everything I had to say into a text. I just told her about Aimi having interest from a music scout who wanted her mobile number.

Sd she gve it to him? Wot do u thnk?
Luv Laurie xxx

I waited for a reply until my eyes felt heavy with sleep. But none came.

The next morning, I woke up to discover my mobile on the floor beside my bed and then I remembered I'd texted my mum the night before.

'*Please* let there be a reply,' I said to myself as I checked. There was! I read it quickly.

Dear Laurie. Hope UR well and wrkng
hrd. Gd news bout Aimi bt she shdn't
gve out her number. She shd give the
school number. Thn all's official with
Ms Lang.Tell her well done frm us.
Hope it's the start of gr8 thngs for her.
Lts of luv from Mum xxx

I smiled, starting to get excited. Good old Mum. I
should've known she'd come up with a top piece of
advice and I couldn't wait to tell everyone. Getting
dressed quickly, I made my way to the communal
bathroom and saw Aimi brushing her teeth.

'Morning, Aimi,' I said cheerfully, trying to patch
things up after our fight the night before.

She eyed me suspiciously as she finished brushing
her teeth.

'What's with the Lucky Six web site being down?'
she asked me suddenly.

I swallowed hard, knowing I couldn't tell her the
truth without there being another scene. I just
couldn't face it so early in the morning.

'Is it? Oh,' I said. 'Perhaps Noah's making some improvements. You know what he's like – always tinkering around with his mad ideas.'

Aimi looked at me as if she guessed I was lying and I decided it was best to hide my face over the basin and have a wash.

Aimi was fiddling around with her hair when I finished.

'Listen, Aimi,' I began. 'I've been thinking about that message from Mr Saunders.'

Aimi's eyes narrowed as if I might be about to totally annoy her again.

'What about it?'

I cleared my throat. 'I think the best thing to do is to give him the school's number. He can call you on that. It's much safer, don't you think? And you should really let Ms Lang know what's happening too.'

'You sound just like Elle. Did she put you up to this?'

'No,' I said. 'I thought of it myself.'

I could see that Aimi was thinking about my idea – or rather, my mum's idea.

'So you're not going to try and block my solo career?' Aimi said.

'Aimi!' I said. 'I was *never* trying to do that. None of us was. We all want you to do really well!'

'Really?'

'Of *course*!' I said.

Aimi twisted a strand of dark hair round her fingers. 'You might have a good point,' she said.

'Then you'll give him the school number?' I

asked, relief flooding through me.

'Yeah. I think I will.'

'And you'll let Ms Lang know what's happening?'
I asked.

'Sure,' Aimi said. 'Won't she be proud of me?'

I nodded, thinking it typical of Aimi that she'd be
after praise from Ms Lang now.

Just then, Elle and Marybeth walked in. They'd
obviously heard the tail-end of our conversation
because they had great grins on their faces.

'I think it's the best way forward,' Elle said,
sounding just like a teacher.

'And you're right,' Marybeth said, 'Ms Lang will
be so proud of you.'

I grinned. Marybeth was so good at flattering
people – much better than I was – and Aimi was
beaming, lapping up all the attention she was getting.

As Aimi left the bathroom, the rest of us huddled
together.

'Well done, Laurie,' Elle said. 'Good work.'

'It'll be much safer this way,' Marybeth said. 'I'm
so relieved she didn't give her number out to that

strange man. I don't trust him.'

'Me neither,' I said. 'And this way everything goes through the school.'

'It's all above board now,' Elle agreed.

'And we can get the web site back up again,' I said. 'I'll tell Noah as soon as poss.' We gave each other a quick hug, and I left the bathroom with a little skip in my step.

Chapter
Six

Ms Diamond's singing classes are always inspirational. She's definitely one of my favourite teachers at the academy. She's still young enough to love all the new artists in the charts and be able to hold a conversation with us students about what's going on in the real world of music (unlike our dinosaur parents and some of the older members of staff).

We had just started a vocal training class, Miss Diamond's caramel curls bobbing in time to our warm-up scales, when Aimi arrived late, which was really unlike her. She usually hated missing the start of classes and was always there early. But what was even more disturbing was the evil look she shot me as she came in. What had I done now?

I thought everything was back to normal again since I'd passed on my mum's good advice to her. I couldn't think what she could be freaking out about this time. All through class I tried to get her attention, but she completely ignored me and I had to wait until the lesson was over to find out what was wrong.

She might have been the last to arrive, but she was the first to leave and I had to catch up with her in the corridor outside.

'Aimi?' I called, pushing through the other students in my attempt to catch up with her. 'What's the matter? What was with that Lady Macbeth look back in class?' We'd been doing Shakespeare's *Macbeth* in English and I thought Aimi would make the perfect leading lady right now.

She stopped, her hands on her hips.

'Ms Lang – *that's* what's wrong.'

I frowned. 'What do you mean?'

'She had a phone call from Mr Saunders.'

'Well, that's good, isn't it?' I asked.

'No, it isn't,' Aimi said, her face like a thunderous cloud. 'I got a right telling off for handing out my CD to a total stranger. She sounded just like you lot. She was furious. And I nearly got suspended for it too, thanks to your brilliant idea.'

'Oh, Aimi,' I said, really upset by this news. 'I thought this was the best thing to do. I thought –'

'Well, you thought wrong, didn't you? You and your smart ideas.'

'Don't be like that,' I said. 'It's not the end of the world.'

'Isn't it? Well, for your information, Ms Lang's barred us from entering the battle-of-the-bands competition.'

My mouth dropped open. 'What?'

'Lucky Six aren't allowed to play, full stop. It was her brilliant idea that I should tell you all. I expect she thought it would make me feel sorry for what I've done, but I don't.'

It was at this point that Elle – who'd also been in our vocal-training class – joined us.

'What's going on?' she asked, and I could see that she looked nervous. Perhaps she thought Aimi and I were about to have another argument, which is what I thought was going to happen too, I don't mind telling you. I quickly filled her in on the latest developments.

'You've got to be kidding,' she said, her face falling in despair at the news. 'But we've been rehearsing like mad.'

'I know,' I said.

'All for nothing,' Aimi said, but I couldn't help thinking that she didn't sound sad about it at all. She sounded totally smug, if anything.

'There must be a way round this,' I said.

'I doubt it,' Aimi said. 'And I really don't care anyway, because it won't affect me.'

'What do you mean?' I asked, my heart in my mouth.

'I don't really care about the stupid competition because I was going to leave Lucky Six anyway.'

'Aimi, how can you say that?' I asked.

'After all we've been through,' Elle said. 'You can't just walk out on us.'

'Watch me,' Aimi said. 'Mr Saunders is obviously planning something for me, and my solo career could be just about to take off. You watch and see.'

'Aimi, wait –' Elle said, as Aimi waltzed off down the corridor.

She stopped and turned back to look at us. 'I'll think of you when I'm rich and famous,' she said, and then turned the corner and disappeared. Elle and I stared after her, open-mouthed. There was nothing left to say.

I couldn't calm down after this latest outburst from Aimi. I was just fuming. Who did she think she was, treating everybody like that and thinking only of herself? And I was becoming more and more convinced that there was a connection between the mysterious Mr Saunders and the break-in at the Akitas' home in Japan. There had to be – right? This was more than pure coincidence, I was sure of it.

That lunchtime, I called a band meeting in the Clubhouse (aka the trunk room). The trunk room was exactly that – a storage area for the boarders' luggage – but we used it as a secret hideaway when we needed to discuss mysteries in private without being interrupted by the likes of nasty Sasha Quinn-Jones having a nosy moment. It was pretty dusty and cold down there, but at least there was lighting and we could get a bit of privacy. So, after wolfing down our lunch in the school canteen, we headed to the Clubhouse to discuss the latest developments.

'She's absolutely furious,' I began, talking about Aimi who, of course, wasn't there. It was beginning to look like we'd have to rename the band Lucky Five before too long. 'Apparently, Ms Lang really laid into her.'

'This is terrible!' Marybeth said, shocked by the news.

'I suppose Ms Lang was only trying to protect Aimi,' Elle said, sounding as grown up as ever. 'You said yourself that it was the best thing for her to do.'

'I know,' I cried, 'but I had no idea Ms Lang would react like this. What do we do now? She's barred us from entering the battle-of-the-bands competition.'

Noah's eyes doubled in size. 'No way!'

'*Way!*' I said. 'It's her way of punishing us for going behind her back.'

'But *we* didn't do anything,' Jack complained. 'It's so unfair!'

'Do you think she'll change her mind?' Marybeth asked.

'I shouldn't think so,' I said, knowing how strict Ms Lang could be. 'I think she wants to make an example of us as a warning to other students who might think of doing the same thing.'

'And how's Aimi taken it?' Marybeth asked.

'She blames me,' I said. 'And she said she's leaving Lucky Six again.'

Jack kicked an empty suitcase in front of him. 'She's always saying that,' he said. 'Just ignore her. She's only trying to get everyone's attention like the drama queen she is.'

Even though we never see eye to eye, I couldn't help grinning at Jack's simple statement because part of it was true. But he hadn't seen Aimi's fury when she'd told me she was leaving the band.

We sat in silence for a few moments, each of us with an unhappy face. As far as we were concerned, life wasn't worth living if we couldn't play our music and win competitions, and the battle of the bands was one of the best competitions around.

Just as I thought things couldn't get any worse, Aimi walked in.

'Aimi!' Marybeth yelled, expressing everyone's surprise to see her.

I bit my lip. What was she doing here? I wondered, instantly suspicious. Was she here to apologise? Was she going to say she'd made a huge mistake in threatening to leave Lucky Six? We didn't have long to find out. She waltzed in as bold as brass and sat down opposite us all as if she were a queen. Ha! Lady Macbeth again, I thought quietly to myself.

'What is it, Aimi?' Noah asked, with a long sigh.

'Yeah, I thought you'd left the band,' Jack said. 'And this is a private band meeting, if you hadn't noticed.'

'Don't worry,' Aimi said, 'I'm not going to stay long. I've got tons to do in preparation for my solo career. I can't be hanging around in luggage all day.'

'So, what do you want?' I asked, my eyes narrowing.

'I've just sent a private message to Mr Saunders, if you must know and, this time, I've given him my mobile number.'

There was a collective gasp of horror from us all.

'What was I supposed to do?' Aimi continued. 'Ms Lang's refused to help me and I'm not turning down an opportunity like this.'

'But, Aimi!' Marybeth cried. 'It might not be an

opportunity at all. It's probably some sort of scam. I thought we'd all decided that.'

'*I* didn't decide that at all,' Aimi said. 'You guys thought one thing and I thought something different.'

'But you've completely ignored every bit of our advice!' Elle said.

'Why on earth did you come to us all worried if you were just going to go behind our backs?' I cried.

'I only went behind your backs because your advice was selfish,' Aimi yelled at me.

'I don't believe how childish you're being, Aimi, I really don't,' I said, feeling my face heating up as I got more and more angry.

Suddenly, everyone was shouting at once.

'You've ruined our chances in the competition,' Jack bellowed.

'This is so dangerous,' Elle cried.

'You should've come to us first,' Marybeth yelled.

'We're all in for it when Ms Lang finds out about

this,' Noah said.

But one voice could be heard above all the others: mine. Mrs D'Silva has always said I can project well.

'You've let us all down, Aimi!' I cried. 'This isn't exactly the team spirit we agreed on for Lucky Six, is it? We're meant to be a band – and band members look after each other. We don't go behind each others' backs and do what we want. You're totally irresponsible and you're going to get yourself expelled if you're not careful. And your parents are going to be furious.'

Aimi just sat staring at us all, a big smirk on her face that made me want to fly at her in rage.

'You are *such* a busybody, Lauren,' Aimi said. 'And that theory of yours about Mr Saunders and my parents' break-in is complete rubbish. You should just stay out of other people's business.'

'It's *everybody's* business now,' I retorted, and then I took a deep breath. This was ridiculous. What had happened to us? 'Look,' I said, calmer now. 'All you need to do is apologise. It's not too late to fix this.'

For a moment, all was quiet as we waited for Aimi to answer. But she wasn't going to say sorry to anyone – no way. Instead, she got up and stormed out of the Clubhouse, leaving us gaping in disbelief after her.

Chapter Seven

'I don't believe it!' I said, as the door slammed behind Aimi. 'Who does she think she is, talking to us like that?'

'Laurie, we've got to try to calm down,' Elle said.

'I don't want to calm down,' I said, pacing up and down the room between the dusty trunks.

'Things are really getting out of control,' Marybeth said. 'But Elle's right – we've got to keep on top of things or we're all gonna land ourselves in big trouble.'

Noah and Jack sat in silence as us girls tried to work things out.

'I'm just so stressed about everything,' I said. 'Aimi, her parents, this Mr Saunders, the competition, Ms Lang.'

'We know,' Elle said. 'We're *all* stressed.'

'And there *must* be a connection between Mr Saunders and the break-in in Japan. I mean, why else would he be so keen to get Aimi's mobile number?'

Everyone was looking at me.

'Don't you get it?' I said. 'It all ties up. The fake record label and the way he just *happened* to appear after the failed break-in at Aimi's parents' place at a time when they were working on this ground-breaking gadget. It's *got* to be connected – I'm sure of it.'

Jack looked up at me. He knew when I was on to something. I was like Mister Binks with a bone – I just wouldn't let go.

'You could be right,' he said. 'It's definitely suspicious.'

'Of course it is, Wart-face!' I said, relieved that I was finally being listened to.

'It's too scary to even think about,' Marybeth said, 'but you make it sound possible, Laurie.'

Elle shook her head. 'I'm not so sure,' she said.

'These things happened on the other side of the world.'

'The world's not so small these days,' Jack pointed out.

'Especially in the world of crime,' I said, rubbing my nose.

'Still,' Elle said, 'Aimi shouldn't be giving her mobile number out to complete strangers. She's an idiot even to think of doing something like that. It's not safe.'

I looked across the room at Noah. He was sitting

with his shoulders slumped and his eyes cast down on the floor. He was the only one who hadn't said anything since Aimi's outburst.

'What do you think, Noah?' I asked.

He shrugged. 'I don't really know what's going on,' he said, with a sigh.

'None of us does,' I said. 'Not *really*.'

'I just want things to go back to normal again,' he said, his voice filled with frustration.

'We all do, Noah,' Marybeth said.

'What's happening here?' he asked. 'Lucky Six doesn't seem to exist any more! One minute we're all buddies and working like crazy for the battle of the bands and the next –' He paused and his silence said it all.

'I know,' I said, sitting down next to him, wondering if I should put an arm round his shoulders. 'Everything's gone wrong. But we've *got* to make sure no one gets hurt. We can't give up just like that. We've worked too hard and we *are* all friends. We've just got to work everything out.'

Everyone nodded in agreement and Noah let out

another huge sigh. Life for Lucky Six was getting way too complicated for his liking, I could tell.

'You know what?' Jack said.

'What?' we all chorused.

'I think we should tell Mr and Mrs Akita to reprogamme their combination.'

I nodded enthusiastically, secretly kicking myself that Jack had come up with this idea before me. 'Yeah, we should,' I said.

'Definitely,' Elle said. 'And straight away.'

'But so that we don't spook them about Aimi's safety,' Jack added. 'You know what parents are like.'

Everyone nodded. The last thing we wanted on our hands was a parent panic.

'Do you think Ms Lang should know too?' Marybeth asked. 'About what Aimi's done?'

I nodded again. 'I think so. She needs to deal with it, I suppose.'

We all looked at each other. At least we'd made some progress.

The lesson bell rang, startling us all back into the

reality that we were at school with lessons to attend. Our plans would have to wait.

I've never known an afternoon to drag by so slowly. For once, I didn't enjoy any of my classes. Maths was a total bore and I just couldn't concentrate in contemporary dance because I couldn't stop thinking about Jack's idea about emailing Mr and Mrs Akita. Once I get an idea in my head, I just want to roll with it – right away. Finally, though, we were all together again – well, five of us anyway – and Jack told us what had been going on.

'I've been doing a bit of sleuthing of my own,' he said.

'You, *sleuthing*?' I said sarcastically.

'Yeah, me,' he said. 'You're not the only one with police for parents.'

I stuck my tongue out at him. He was so annoying sometimes.

'So, what happened?' Elle asked, trying to steer

Jack back on course.

Jack gave me a silly smug grin and continued. 'Well, you know Aimi's not speaking to us and I needed to get her parents' email address? So I went on to the Lucky Six web site and looked at the message board. It didn't take long to find a message from them and hit respond.'

'Cool,' Noah said. 'I'd never have thought of that.'

'I know,' Jack teased him, and Noah grinned back.

'So, what did you say, Wart-face?' I asked.

'That Aimi said they were working on a really important project. I said how exciting it must be. And then I found this link on the Internet – a report that warned people about the importance of changing the combinations on their locks.'

'Good thinking, Jack,' Elle said.

I bristled at her praise of my little brother but realised he'd done well – for him.

'Do you think that'll do the trick?' Jack asked.

'I hope so,' I said. 'I really hope so.'

And then it was time for Elle, Marybeth and me to tell Ms Lang what had been happening. We felt really terrible heading over to her office,.

'I feel like a traitor!' Marybeth said.

'Me too,' Elle said. 'I don't want to drop Aimi in it or anything.'

'But we have to let Ms Lang know what's going on,' I said. 'It's the right thing to do. It has to be – it's for Aimi's own safety.'

'But what if she gets suspended?' Marybeth said. 'I'll feel just awful.'

'Me too,' Elle said.

'Me three,' I said. 'But we can't worry about that now. We've got to face one problem at a time.'

When we arrived at Ms Lang's office, we were all suddenly very nervous. Were we doing the right thing? I looked at Elle and Marybeth for reassurance, but they were looking at me for exactly the same thing. None of us wanted to be there. But it was the only thing we could do – right?

'You knock, Laurie,' Elle said.

I might've known it would be down to me,

I thought. I took a deep breath, counted to three, and knocked.

We waited. And waited.

'Knock again,' Marybeth whispered. 'Louder.'

I did, and we waited once again.

'It's no good,' I said. 'She's not in.'

Just then, Mrs Walsh walked by.

'Hello, girls,' she said. 'Can I help you?'

'We wanted to speak to Ms Lang,' I said.

'Oh, well, she's out walking Mister Binks,' Mrs Walsh said. Elle, Marybeth and I obviously looked disappointed. 'Is there anything I can help you with?' We stood shuffling our feet and looking nervous. 'If you've come to try and change her mind about the battle-of-the-bands competition, I don't think you're going to have much luck.'

We all opened our mouths at once to start explaining, but at that second Aimi appeared, heading down the corridor right towards us.

'Oh,' I said quickly, 'no, Mrs Walsh. It's OK. There's no problem.'

'It can wait,' Marybeth chipped in.

'Nothing to worry about,' Elle added, just as Aimi walked past. I tried not to flinch as she completely blanked us, but Mrs Walsh obviously noticed that there was something going on between us – in fact, it would have been virtually impossible to miss. She gave us a puzzled look.

'Well,' she said, 'if you're absolutely sure everything's OK.'

'Oh, yes, Mrs Walsh,' I said brightly. 'Everything's fine.'

She looked at us again and then, to our great relief, went on her way.

'Blimey, that was close,' Elle said, as we watched Mrs Walsh heading in one direction and Aimi in the other.

'Do you think Aimi realised what we were up to?' Marybeth asked.

'I shouldn't have thought so,' I said. 'She only seems to be interested in herself at the moment.

With that, we headed back to my room, but on the way we passed Aimi in the corridor. She was talking to Jess Wiseman – a girl in our year – and

she obviously knew that we were there because her voice was raised deliberately so we'd all hear what she was saying.

'I'm so looking forward to it,' she said, tossing her dark hair over her shoulder. 'I'm meeting with Mr Saunders tomorrow evening. It's all arranged. And we'll be talking about my solo career – isn't that exciting?'

Jess nodded. What choice did she have, poor girl?

'Yes,' Aimi continued, 'I can't believe it's actually happening after all I've been through trying to get this sorted out. You won't believe the hassle it's been because of so-called friends interfering.' Aimi casually checked her nails and then went on. 'But it was about time I left Lucky Six. They were just holding me back.'

Elle, Marybeth and I stared at Aimi in horror as she continued.

'So,' she said, 'if you know of anyone who'd like to take my place in the band, they're welcome to it. I certainly won't miss it.'

'Sure, Aimi,' Jess said.

'Put the news about, won't you?' Aimi said. 'There's a vacancy for a guitarist in Lucky Six.'

We'd heard more than enough and went to my room, closing the door behind us.

'Can you believe her?' I said. I was so angry that she'd say such things about us.

'I'm ready to believe anything now,' Elle said, looking deeply depressed by the whole thing.

'So what do we do?'

I sighed. 'Well, we failed to tell Ms Lang about it and I'm not sure that was such a good idea anyway. I think it was too risky and I don't know what we'd have done if we got Aimi expelled.'

We sat in silence for a while and then I said, 'We're going to have to try and speak to Aimi ourselves.'

Elle and Marybeth looked anxious.

'But she hasn't taken our advice about anything,' Marybeth said.

'I know,' I said. 'But we have to try to stop her from meeting this Mr Saunders. I don't think we've got any other choice.'

Chapter Eight

It was a totally frustrating day. Elle, Marybeth and I tried our very best to speak to Aimi and warn her off meeting with Mr Saunders but she completely avoided any contact with us and I'm sure she knew we were trying to talk to her.

'I've lost count of the number of texts I've sent her,' Elle complained, and I nodded because I'd sent more than my fair share too.

'And she's not answering her phone either,' Marybeth said.

It was a wonder the three of us hadn't been driven completely mad by this stage. We were all trying so hard to make sure Aimi was safe but she was too pig-headed even to listen to us.

When I got back to my room, I was seriously

shattered. For a moment, I lay on my bed and closed my eyes, wishing – like Noah – that everything would just go back to normal. I missed Aimi's company: her laughter and sense of fun, her passion for the band. But she'd changed and I was beginning to worry that we'd never see the old Aimi again.

It was then that I received a text from Jack and it was good news. He'd heard back from Mr and Mrs Akita. They'd emailed him to thank him for his tip-off about the combination lock number. What they'd told him next made my heart race: they'd had another attempted break-in at their office but, thankfully, the thieves were unsuccessful again. Honestly, my heart was in my mouth as I read more. The Akitas had gone on to say that their ground-breaking gadget had since been moved to another location for safety's sake.

I breathed a sigh of relief at this news and I couldn't help feeling a little bit pleased too because I'd just *known* my hunch had been right. I've got supersleuth skill when it comes to mysteries! Mr Saunders and the thieves in Japan *were* linked somehow. All we had to do now was find out how, and what exactly they were up to.

'OK,' I told myself, as I climbed off my bed. 'Calm down. This is the best news ever because it proves you were right but you've still got to prove it to Aimi.' I groaned. That wasn't going to be easy, I knew, but I had to give it a try.

I ran out of my room and down the corridor to Aimi's room to show her Jack's text with the news about her parents' second break-in.

'Aimi?' I called, banging on the door. 'It's me – Laurie. Let me in. I've got some really important news.' I waited a moment and then knocked again.

'Aimi? I know you're angry with me but you've got to listen. This is important. Open the door.' I banged again but there was still no answer. It meant only one thing – I was too late. Aimi had obviously left already to meet Mr Saunders.

In a mad panic, I opened the door. 'Aimi?' I said, quietly this time, but my suspicions were right – the room was empty. I gulped with fear at what this meant.

Without a moment's pause, I ran back down the corridor, my mind whirling madly. I knew what I had to do, though. First stop: Elle's.

'Laurie? What is it?' she asked from her desk where she was doing her homework when I crashed, unannounced, into her room.

'Aimi's gone,' was all I could manage, the words gasping out of me.

'Gone – where?'

'To meet Mr Saunders. I tried to stop her but I was too late. She'd already left. And the Akitas have had another break-in, Elle,' I blurted. 'It's all linked. I was right, and now Aimi's gone and she's in danger, I just know it.'

'Right!' Elle said, leaping out of her chair. 'Let's get Marybeth.'

Marybeth was as dumbstruck as we were when I told her what had happened. 'What do we do?' she asked hopelessly, her violet eyes wide with concern.

I took a deep breath. 'I think we have to go back to Ms Lang.'

We all looked at each other and realised that, even though this was the last thing we wanted to do, Aimi had left us no other choice.

When we knocked this time, there *was* an answer, thank goodness.

'Come in,' Ms Lang called, and we opened the door and entered the room. Almost immediately, Mister Binks started yapping.

'Quiet!' Ms Lang commanded, and the dog was instantly silent. 'Hello, Lauren,' she said. 'And Elle and Marybeth.' She looked at us all as she motioned for us to sit down. 'I do hope you girls aren't wasting my time by trying to persuade me to change my mind about the battle of the bands because I can tell you that it won't do any good whatsoever.'

'Oh, no, Ms Lang,' I said quickly. 'I wish it *was* that.'

Ms Lang stared at me. 'Then what is it, Lauren?'

'It's far more serious than the band,' I continued, never thinking I'd admit that anything was more serious than Lucky Six doing well.

'Well, you'd better tell me, then,' Ms Lang said, and so I went right back to the beginning. I told her all about Mr Saunders, the business card, how

we could find no trace of him on the Internet, how Aimi's room being broken into seemed connected to the break-in at the Akitas', Aimi not listening to us and giving out her mobile number – the Akitas' combination lock, the more recent break-in at their house that followed and, lastly, the fact that Aimi had arranged to meet Mr Saunders and was now nowhere to be found.

By the time I'd finished, I was pretty breathless. I looked at Ms Lang. Her lips were pressed so tight they'd virtually disappeared.

'You do believe me?' I asked, terrified that she was going to think I'd made the whole thing up to get Aimi into trouble.

Ms Lang nodded slowly.

'Do you mean to tell me that not only has Aimi disobeyed me, but she has broken the school rules as well?' she said quietly. She paused and looked at us gravely. 'You have all put Aimi at risk for not reporting this sooner.'

'But, Ms Lang,' I interrupted, 'that's not fair. We've tried to stop Aimi every step of the way. And we didn't really know what was going on until Jack got the text from the Akitas about the second break-in.'

'And we hoped Aimi would listen to us,' Elle said, springing to my defence.

'We knew her parents would be really ashamed if she was suspended from the academy,' I said, 'or, worse, expelled, and Lucky Six would've lost a band member.'

I looked at Elle and Marybeth. They were both

white-faced and I was sure I was too.

'We need to find Aimi,' Ms Lang said, 'and fast.'

We watched as she reached for the phone.

Chapter Nine

Ms Lang didn't get the chance to make a call because, just as she was about to pick up the receiver, it rang, making us all jump.

Ms Lang picked up the phone. 'Hello. Verity Lang Academy.' She frowned. 'Mr Akita?'

We all sat forward in our chairs, desperate to hear what was being said. What if they'd had another break-in? What if the thieves had got the gadget this time? My mind raced as I tried to imagine what was being said.

Finally, Ms Lang put the phone down and turned to look at us.

'Well,' she said, 'it seems you girls were right to be worried. Mr and Mrs Akita are extremely concerned that the thieves who broke into their house will stop at nothing to get hold of their gadget. They're especially concerned about Aimi and have asked me to be extra-vigilant, which, I must say, is particularly difficult when you girls have not kept me informed.'

I opened my mouth to protest, but Ms Lang's attention was suddenly drawn to the door which was slightly ajar. I turned round to follow her gaze and saw Aimi. She looked wide-eyed and frightened and she was obviously trying to sneak past the office without being noticed, probably aware that she was in big trouble.

'Aimi!' Ms Lang called out in a sing-song voice. 'Come here.' Cautiously, Aimi obeyed, entering the office slowly. 'I've just been speaking with your parents and I think they'd like to talk with you,' she said, tapping the number into the phone and handing the receiver to Aimi. 'And *I'll* have a word with you later, young lady,' she added with a dark glower.

We all listened as Aimi spoke to her parents in Japanese, probably telling them that she was OK

100

and that they didn't have to worry about her – you know, the kind of stuff kids always tell their parents when they're in trouble. Finally, Aimi hung up the phone and looked anxiously at Ms Lang.

'Young lady,' she began, 'I have a good mind to expel you for what you've done. Have you any idea what you've put us all through? Your friends, your family, your school? Your behaviour has been completely unacceptable.'

Aimi looked down at the carpet miserably and I couldn't help feeling sorry for her.

'However,' Ms Lang continued, and I held my breath. *However* sounded positive, didn't it? *However* held hope. 'However,' she said again, 'I am under the impression that you have probably learned your lesson already.'

Everyone breathed a huge sigh of relief and I could see Aimi begin to relax.

'And, of course, I don't want to cause your parents any more stress. They've been through quite enough already.'

Aimi had the good sense to look upset. 'I'm so sorry, Ms Lang,' she said. 'I'm sorry for all the worry I've caused everyone.'

Ms Lang nodded.

'I can't believe what's happened,' Aimi continued. 'I feel like such an idiot.' She bit her lip and I was sure there were tears swimming in her dark eyes. 'Mr Saunders was never interested in me or my music,' she said in a small voice.

'Oh, Aims,' I said, feeling her anguish.

'All he wanted to know about was my parents' new gadget. He kept asking me where it was. He went on and on, and when I wouldn't tell him anything, he tried to –'

'What?' we all said in unison.

'He tried to bundle me into his car.'

'Aimi!' I moaned.

'Oh, Aims!' Elle cried.

'You poor thing,' Marybeth whispered.

Ms Lang's face burned a startling scarlet.

'How did you get away?' I asked.

Aimi gave a tiny smile. 'I kicked him in the shins and ran for it.'

I shuddered, thinking how awful it could've been – what might have happened – if Aimi hadn't got away from him.

'He tried to kidnap you, Aimi,' I said.

Ms Lang took a deep breath. 'Aimi, you will be grounded for the next month. You will have to report to me every morning before classes and every afternoon after classes so I can confidently reassure your parents that I am keeping an eye on you. This is, after all, what they've requested.'

'Yes, Ms Lang,' Aimi agreed sheepishly, and I couldn't help thinking that she'd got off lightly – with everything.

'Now,' Ms Lang said, sitting forward at her enormous desk and steepling her fingers together, 'I have a plan.'

We looked at one another.

'What kind of plan?' I couldn't resist asking.

'A plan to catch this Mr Saunders,' Ms Lang said, one delicate eyebrow raised slightly. 'Of course, it will mean that Lucky Six will have to play at the battle of the bands.'

For a moment, we didn't quite believe what she was saying. We could play in the competition? Help solve a mystery? It sounded too good to be true.

Ms Lang went on to explain. 'If Mr Saunders really is after Aimi, of which I have no doubt whatsoever, then he will be there on the night, don't you agree?'

We nodded.

'Right,' Ms Lang said. 'We have work to do. I shall contact the police and make sure Mr Saunders is dealt with.'

We looked at each other again and I couldn't help feeling the stirrings of excitement. We were about to be launched into a real-life mystery!

'All right, girls, you may leave. I think you'll have plenty of rehearsing to do, not so?' she said, dismissing us with a wave of her hand before reaching for the telephone once again.

We left the office and, outside in the corridor, we met Mrs Walsh.

'Aimi!' she said with relief in her voice. She stepped forward and gave Aimi a big hug. 'You had us all so worried! Are you all right?'

Aimi managed a weak smile. 'I'm fine, Mrs Walsh,' she said.

'Good,' Mrs Walsh said. 'You make sure you take good care of yourself, OK?'

Aimi nodded and Mrs Walsh gave a big sigh before leaving us.

'Oh, Aimi!' Elle said. 'She's right, you know.

We've been so worried about you.'

'You were?'

'Of course we were, you idiot,' I said. 'You should never have left us like that.'

'We were all freaked out about you, you ninny,' Marybeth said. 'You must promise you'll never do anything that crazy again.'

Suddenly, we were having a huge group hug right in the middle of the corridor.

'Can you believe we're back in the running for

the battle-of-the-bands competition?' I said.

'Tomorrow!' Marybeth screamed.

'We've got some serious work ahead of us,' Elle said. 'We're really under-rehearsed.'

'Oh, Elle! Don't be such a worrier. We'll be fine,' I said with a laugh. I was just so relieved that things were slowly returning to normal again. 'Wait until Noah and Jack hear. They'll be so pleased.'

We looked at Aimi, who was looking miserable again.

'Aren't you pleased, Aimi?' Marybeth asked.

'Of course I am,' she said, her eyes cast to the floor. 'It's just – well – I feel so stupid. I've behaved really badly.'

'It's OK,' I said. 'We still love you. Lucky Six just wouldn't be the same without Aimi to keep us on our toes.'

Aimi sighed. 'Can you forgive me?' she asked in a small voice, her dark eyes looking up at us all.

'Of course we forgive you!' I said.

'You crazy person!' Marybeth said, hugging

Aimi again.

'Forgiven and forgotten,' Elle said.

'Er, well, not quite forgotten,' I said. 'We've still got to get through tomorrow night.'

'I should've listened to all your warnings,' Aimi said. 'I can't believe how foolish I've been.'

'You must've been terrified when Mr Saunders tried to force you into his car,' Elle said. 'I only hope we catch him.'

We all nodded.

'By the way,' Aimi said, 'I've worked out what's missing from my room.'

'You mean, what was taken in the break-in?' I said.

Aimi nodded. 'It was a bundle of letters from my parents. I think Mr Saunders must have sneaked on to campus and taken them.'

'Perhaps he thought there might be some clue to how to get his hands on your parents' new gadget?' I asked, rubbing my nose.

'I guess,' Aimi said. 'But I'm not that stupid and neither are my parents. We wouldn't write that sort of stuff in a letter.' Aimi suddenly blushed. 'But I was stupid enough to give him my mobile number. I can't believe I did that.'

'It's all in the past now,' Elle said.

'And look at the positive side,' I said.

'What's that?'

'At least when the next criminal poses as a talent scout and asks for your mobile number, you'll be totally prepared!' I said, and then laughed. Everyone else laughed too.

'Thank you, guys, for letting me back in Lucky Six,' Aimi said. 'You're good friends.' Her eyes glimmered.

'Well, we're just thankful that we won't have to hold endless auditions to find a replacement,' Elle grinned. 'Imagine what that would've been like,' she said, rolling her eyes.

'And nobody could replace you, anyway,' Marybeth added.

'I can't believe we'll all be playing again tomorrow night,' I said.

'On one condition,' Aimi said.

We looked at her. 'What?' we asked.

'That we can play one of my songs,' Aimi replied, a cheeky grin slowly spreading across her face.

We laughed out loud. It was good to have her back.

Chapter
Ten

True to her word, Ms Lang rang the police and, first thing on Saturday morning, a male and female police officer came to the academy to talk to the band. Of course, Jack and I were totally unfazed by the whole experience even if everyone else at the academy was gobsmacked. Having police for parents, we were used to it all but I still enjoyed telling them everything.

'That's when I just *knew* the two break-ins had to be linked,' I said as we all related the extraordinary events of the past few weeks.

'And then I got a text from the Akitas saying they'd had another attempted burglary,' Jack said importantly. 'They thanked me for warning them and told me they'd changed their security details.'

'But Mr Saunders wouldn't give up,' Elle said. 'And Aimi wasn't to know he was up to no good.'

'Oh, I can't believe I gave him my mobile number,' Aimi said, her head in her hands.

'And that was the number your parents used for their combination?' the policewoman asked, checking her notes.

'Yes,' Aimi said. 'And then I went to meet him.'

We were all silent for a moment as Aimi retold her story.

'It was really scary. He tried to grab me and push me into his car, but I kicked him – really hard – and ran and ran.'

'You did very well,' the policewoman said.

'But I was seriously terrified,' Aimi said, her eyes wide and her hair flying about her face as she looked around the room at everyone, making sure she had everybody's attention. 'It was the most nerve-wracking experience anyone could have – *ever*!'

I rolled my eyes. I knew this whole thing must've been really traumatic for Aimi, but I couldn't help thinking she was hamming it up a

bit. But, then again, that was Aimi – always happiest in the limelight and I couldn't really begrudge her her moment after all she'd been through.

'Well,' the policeman said, after hearing our story, 'I must say that I'm very impressed with your sleuthing skills. Very impressed indeed. All of you.'

I beamed with pride, knowing that Lucky Six was a great team, even if it had taken a while for me to convince everyone that I was right. It had all come good in the end, hadn't it?

'In fact,' the policewoman said, 'if you ever decide that the music industry isn't for you, then my colleague and I could well be out of our jobs!'

We laughed.

'Perhaps you should wait and see us perform in the battle-of-the-bands competition this afternoon before you make your minds up,' I said, knowing that although I loved solving mysteries my music would always come first.

They smiled and nodded.

'We're looking forward to it very much,' the policewoman said, and then the policeman cleared his throat and went on to explain how things would work later that day at the Lowfield Shopping Centre.

'There'll be plain-clothes officers in the crowd waiting to catch Mr Saunders. We think it's very likely he'll turn up and make a second attempt to snatch Aimi. He's got access to your whereabouts through your web site.'

Noah tutted. 'I was wondering if we should've taken that down again.'

'You can't blame yourself,' I said quickly, seeing that Noah was looking upset and angry.

'And it's our publicity,' Elle said. 'We need it.'

'You're right,' the policewoman said, 'you can't change your lives because of this one man.'

'So we just want to assure you that we'll be ready for him,' the policeman went on. 'We think it's his plan to use Aimi as some kind of bargaining chip, and force Mr and Mrs Akita into giving him the gadget they're working on.'

'You mean try to kidnap her again?' I said.

Aimi's mouth dropped open in horror.

'Oh, Aimi!' Marybeth said.

'Don't worry,' the policeman said. 'We won't let that happen. He won't get near you.'

'But what a low-down, sneaky, nasty thing to do,' I said, and I couldn't help but notice that Noah and Jack were grinning at each other, their eyes gleaming. Just like boys to get excited by such things, I thought. Elle and Marybeth gulped and

Aimi's face was a mixture of alarm and defiance. And what about me? How did I feel about all this? Well, after all he'd put us through, I had to try and stop myself from actually rubbing my hands together at the idea of the nasty Mr Saunders getting his comeuppance at long last . . .

After what seemed like an absolute age, the battle-of-the-bands competition was finally in full swing. Lucky Six were on last so we were all hanging out in our dressing room, desperately trying to calm our nerves. Well, everyone but me. My mind was racing with the anticipation of performing *and* the thought of Mr Saunders being caught. It was all I could do to remain sitting in my seat. But, when someone knocked at the door, I almost leaped right out of it.

'Come in,' I called, wondering who it could be.

'Well, if it isn't Unlucky Six,' a voice said, and Sasha Quinn-Jones entered the dressing room, looking ridiculous in a tight, frilly dress she'd probably seen some supermodel wearing in a magazine and hadn't bothered checking if it would actually *suit* her.

'What are you doing here, Sasha?' I asked.

'Just come to wish you good luck,' she said, her cold eyes focusing on Noah.

'Yeah, right,' I said.

'Feeling a little stressed, Laurie?' Sasha responded. She tossed her long blonde hair over her shoulder and gave me a sickly sort of smile, like a crocodile might before it was about to bite you. 'What were those police doing at the school, anyway?'

'None of your business,' Aimi said.

'They were the fashion police,' Jack said, pointing to her ridiculous dress, 'asking us if we knew of any victims.'

Sasha's mouth dropped open. 'I've *got* fashion sense, unlike *some* people,' she said, staring pointedly at Marybeth, who blushed and turned away.

'Marybeth looks great,' I said. I really hate it when Sasha starts to pick on Marybeth. Sasha may

117

have a problem with her being a scholarship student, but Marybeth's got twenty times her talent – and Sasha knows it.

'Great?' she sneered. 'You think?'

'Shut it, Sasha,' Jack said.

'Yeah,' Elle said, 'you'd better leave. You shouldn't be backstage at all.'

'In trouble again, are you?' she said. 'I bet the police came to warn you not to play any of your rubbish music or they'd arrest you.'

Suddenly, Jack sprang up and, before Sasha could say another word, he'd pushed her out of the room and shut the door in her face.

'Nice one, Jack,' Noah said, and the rest of us giggled.

Things quietened down a bit after that as we all prepared for the stage. I watched as Noah kissed his lucky drumsticks. Aimi, Elle and Marybeth were taking deep breaths and Jack was – well, Jack was being Jack and playing a game on his mobile while eating a packet of smelly crisps. I thought of the long and anxious journey we'd all made to get to this point. The rehearsals, the arguments, the worries, the break-ins, Aimi's near suspension and her even nearer kidnapping. It was a wonder we'd made it here.

I looked round at everyone and couldn't help smiling. Elle looked as polished and gorgeous as ever, her nails a dazzling gold after a do-it-yourself manicure. Aimi was her usual rock-chick cool in denim, her blue-streaked hair loose, and Marybeth was wearing a stunning dress she'd made herself. No wonder she'd caught Sasha's squinty eye! And the boys? Jack was Jack but I had to admit that he looked good tonight in his favourite jeans and a crisp T-shirt that didn't have a single stain on it. And Noah? He looked as incredible as ever – in a crumpled kind of way.

I glimpsed myself in the mirror. I was having a good hair day, thank heavens, and I was really pleased with how I looked in my black dress with the sparkly straps. Yep, I thought, we all looked great!

Finally, the time came for us to be on stage.

'Are we ready?' I said, leaping out of my seat in excitement.

'As ready as we'll ever be,' Elle said.

'Let's show 'em what we're made of,' Jack said.

Marybeth and Aimi nodded and Noah waved his lucky drumsticks above his head.

'Good luck, everyone,' I said, smiling as I opened the dressing-room door and led the band on to the stage. That, for me, has to be the most adrenaline-filled and exhilarating moment, every time. So many thoughts whizzed through my head then. Would everything go all right? Would the audience like us? Would the songs go down well? And tonight, of course, we had the added worry of Mr Saunders. What if he didn't show up? What if all the plans were wasted? I couldn't bear the thought of him just being out there in the world, free to do what he wanted. He *had* to be here tonight. Things *had* to go right for us.

We neared the stage and I swear I could hear my heartbeat above the noise of the audience. It was a good crowd and I didn't want to let them down.

And it was then that everything seemed to happen at once.

At first, I didn't even see them, but suddenly two burly men came towards us. I'd spotted them out of the corner of my eye and I'd just assumed they were stagehands – there were always so many people backstage. Then these guys made a grab for Aimi!

Marybeth let out a high-pitched scream and Noah and Jack instantly sprang into action.

'Let her GO!' Noah yelled, as he and Jack tried desperately to pull Aimi away. But the men just held her tightly and, before we could do anything, they'd bundled her out, kicking and screaming, through the front entrance.

'AIMI!' I yelled. 'Someone *help*!' I looked around for someone – *anyone* – but nobody seemed to be doing anything. And it was then that I saw a familiar figure in the crowd – someone short and bald and creepy – and he was making a run for it.

'There he is!' I shouted. 'It's Rich Saunders. And he's getting away!'

We watched as several men emerged from the audience and gave chase, tearing after Mr Saunders through the back exit. They must've been the plain-clothes officers the policeman had told us about.

'Come on, everyone. We've got to follow them,' I cried. 'We've got to go after Aimi. Those men who grabbed her must've been Saunders' henchmen.'

We pushed and pelted our way through the tightly packed audience, my heart thudding wildly. There were so many people and they all seemed to be getting in our way. For a minute, I panicked. We'd never reach her, I thought. She's going to be kidnapped and we'll never see her again. Aimi! We had to get to Aimi!

I decided to play it tough, elbowing my way through the crowds.

'Excuse me!' I yelled, pushing and shoving. 'Let me *through*!' But there were so many people that it seemed to take forever.

Finally, we arrived, panting, outside the venue.

'Where is she?' I shouted.

'Aimi?' Elle called.

'I can't see her,' Marybeth said, a look of horror on her face.

It was then that I saw Jack's eyes widening and he pointed behind us.

Now, I'd just like to point out here how worried I'd been about Aimi. I'd never been so frightened in my entire life and I'd really thought we'd lost her forever. But there she was – looking as if nothing in the world was wrong. There was no kicking or screaming, no cries for help. Aimi was standing laughing and chatting with the two henchmen! Great, huh?

'Aimi!' I cried, my mouth dropping open. 'What on earth's going on?'

Aimi turned and saw us staring at her in bewilderment and suddenly cracked up laughing. 'You idiots!' she said. 'They're both policemen – plain-clothes officers!'

Realisation dawned and I didn't know whether to laugh or cry.

123

'But they grabbed you,' Noah said.

'Of course they did – to save me,' Aimi said smugly, as if she'd been in on their plan all along.

'But you were fooled too,' I said. Aimi nodded.

'I know. I was really terrified. I thought it was Saunders' men for sure but it was the only thing they could do.'

The two men stepped forward and nodded. 'Sorry to scare you all like that. But it was necessary to protect your friend from Mr Saunders. We'd had word that he was out in the audience and ready to make a move.'

'Yes,' I said. 'I saw him. Well, thank goodness you were there when you were and managed to save Aimi.'

'Just imagine if it *had* been Saunders' men that had run off with our Aimi,' Elle said. 'We'd have been in a real gherkin.'

'*Pickle*, Elle!' I said with a grin. Ahhh, Elle, she's always getting phrases like that wrong.

'And right before our performance, too,' Noah said with a grin.

124

'We'd never have stood a chance of winning,' Jack said.

Marybeth sighed, ruffling her blonde curls. 'What a day this has been!'

'That's got to be the understatement of the year!' I said, and we all laughed with relief that Aimi was safe and everything was OK.

But then something occurred to me. Everything wasn't OK, was it?

'Hey,' I said, 'where *is* Rich Saunders?'

Everyone looked around as if expecting to see him still doing a runner.

'Perhaps he's in the audience somewhere,' Jack said.

'Yeah, right,' I said. 'Like that's likely, Pea-brain. He'll have legged it ages ago.'

Just as I'd said that, we saw him. But he wasn't doing a runner. He was being led from the back of the venue by the other plain-clothes officers who had chased him out of the back exit.

'He's been caught!' Marybeth said. 'They've got him.'

We all glared at him as he was pushed into a
waiting police van. Part of me wanted to go up to
him and tell the weasel exactly what I thought of
him – to let him know what he'd put us through –
but I didn't. People like that don't care, do they?
So I just narrowed my eyes in fury and watched as
he was driven away to the station.

'I hope that's the last we see of that creep,'
I said.

'Me too,' Aimi agreed. 'I've had enough

excitement to last a lifetime.'

I turned to look at her. 'I hope not,' I said, 'because we've still got our performance to look forward to.'

We said our farewells and thank yous to the police officers and ran back inside the venue where we were met by rapturous applause from the crowd.

'What's going on?' Noah asked.

'I reckon they think all that police stuff was staged,' I said.

Everyone was clapping and cheering and whistling. It was amazing! They really thought that the crazy goings-on were all part of our performance and – well – we didn't want to spoil things by telling them otherwise, did we?

In no time we took our places back onstage. It felt so good to be there. We were reunited once again and I beamed around at the others as Aimi deftly played the intro to her favourite number. The lights were warm and welcoming and the audience cheered us on.

Lucky Six were back in the competition and better than ever!

FACT FILE STAR SIGNS GUIDE TO... BEAUTY

ELLE

NAME: Elle Beaumont
AGE: 14
STAR SIGN: Virgo
HAIR: Dark brown - cut into a stylish, glossy bob
EYES: Brown
LOVES: Singing, listening to pop CDs, organising
people and going home to France
HATES: Being teased about being a perfectionist
WORST CRINGE EVER: When she organised a big gig
for the band, got everything ready, nagged everyone
to turn up on time (which they did), then she realised
she'd got the date wrong!

FACT FILE · **STAR SIGNS** · GUIDE TO... · BEAUTY

STAR FASHION

READ ON TO SEE WHAT YOUR STAR SIGN IS SHOUTING OUT ABOUT YOUR FASHION STYLE!

ARIES
You're all about having fun, so bright colours rock your world. You can normally be found wowing the crowd in your funkiest T-shirts and trendy jeans.

TAURUS
Being fashionable is super-important to you! Your favourite clothes are whatever the coolest celebs are wearing because you love to be just like them!

GEMINI
Slogan T-shirts are what you're all about because you love to be cheeky with your clothes and your attitude. Jeans and cute skirts complete your style.

CANCER
Comfort is the most important thing to you, so it's tracksuit bottoms, hoodies and vest tops to make you feel totally chilled out!

LEO
Hey, glam gal! You want to get noticed, so your favourite fashions are mini skirts, sparkly tops and all the accessories you can find!

VIRGO
You're a matching madam so you love clothes that totally go together. You're all about wearing cool classics. Who cares what's actually in fashion!

LIBRA
Whatever's lying on your bedroom floor is what you're wearing! You grab what you find first and somehow manage to make it look amazing!

SCORPIO
Who says blue and green should never be seen? You love to break the fashion rules and work your look the way that only you can!

SAGITTARIUS
Sporty styles are what works for you and you could happily wear your trainers all day – even to bed! You're at your best in a tracksuit or swimming costume!

CAPRICORN
Girlie styles totally work best for you. If you could wear dresses, pink skirts and bows every day then you'd be the happiest girl around!

AQUARIUS
Weird and wacky is your look! You wear what you want, how you want. If that means a skirt as a top or tights as gloves then that's cool!

PISCES
Who cares what you wear because you're all about accessories! Hats, scarves, necklaces and hair bits all make you feel like a star!

FACT FILE   STAR SIGNS   GUIDE TO ...   BEAUTY

 MARYBETH'S GUIDE TO SISTERS

WHETHER YOU'VE GOT ONE OR WHETHER YOU ARE ONE YOURSELF, YOU KNOW WHAT TRICKY CUSTOMERS SISTERS CAN BE. COMPLETE THIS MINI-QUIZ AND SEE IF YOUR FEMALE SIBLING IS THE SISTER FROM HELL . . .

- Does she enjoy criticising you?
- Does she spend most of her time sulking?
- Does she snitch on you whenever she can?
- Does she always blame you for everything?
- Does she moan about you being the 'favourite'?
- Does she embarrass you in front of boys?
- Does she always 'borrow' your clothes?

If you answered 'yes' to more than half of these questions, you've got yourself a big sisterly problem! So what now?

MARYBETH'S TIPS

Well, for older sisters you need to treat them with a bit of respect. Mix in some flattery and you are half way to getting them on your side. Younger sisters respond better to straight-talk. Not bullying – that won't help, so just be firm. If the problem is really serious and you feel you can't solve it alone, get some advice from your favourite adult – one with a sister of their own if possible!

FACT FILE STAR SIGNS GUIDE TO... | **BEAUTY**

BEAUTY FOOD !

GIVE YOUR FACE A FOODIE TREAT WITH SOME HOME-MADE SKINCARE RECIPES!

THIS IS A GREAT CLEANSER FOR YOUR SKIN THAT'LL KEEP IT NICE AND SMOOTH . . .

YOU'LL NEED:
- Some oatmeal
- Some milk
- A bowl
- Some water
- A towel

WHAT TO DO:

1. Mix one tablespoon of oatmeal and a few drops of milk in a bowl until it forms a paste

2. Rub into your skin using your fingertips

3. Leave for a few minutes then rinse off with warm water

4. Pat your skin dry with a warm towel

BEAUTY AND THE BEAST!

HAVE FUN CREATING YOUR OWN MONSTER OF POP WITH A LITTLE HELP FROM YOUR FRIENDS!

1) Gather together a bundle of old pop magazines and divide them up between you

2) Each player should go through the magazines and cut out lots of pictures of pop stars' faces. Choose ones that are more or less the same size and the game will work better

3) Cut each head into six pieces – hair, two separate eyes, nose, and mouth. Put all the bits in a pile in front of you. Now you're ready to play pop picture consequences and make your very own pop creations

4) Start by making sure everyone has a piece of blank paper

5) All rummage through your piles of picture bits and select some features from the different piles making sure that they're not matching

6) Use a small dab of glue to stick the hair to the top of your page. Don't go over the edges with the glue or you won't be able to unfold the paper at the end of the game!

7) Try to make the best looking and the ugliest pop collage possible and see who does the best job!

THE YES/NO GAME

DID YOU KNOW THAT IN BULGARIA, A NOD OF THE HEAD MEANS 'NO' AND A SHAKE MEANS 'YES'? TRY ANSWERING THE FOLLOWING QUESTIONS IN BULGARIAN (BY SHAKING YOUR HEAD FOR EVERY YES AND NODDING FOR A NO). HERE'S HOW TO PLAY . . .

WHAT TO DO:
1) Take it in turns
2) If you do it wrong, you're out
3) Make up new questions if any player manages to get the following lot right, and continue asking them until they get in a muddle
4) The winner is the person who can answer the most questions without making a mistake. (Even a slight nod, when it should be a shake, counts as an error!)

QUESTIONS
- Do you have a sister?
- Do you like sprouts?
- Is maths your favourite subject?
- Have you got a dog?
- Do you walk to school?
- Have you got a bike?
- Do you play computer games?
- Is your name Mildred?
- Do you like playing computer games?
- Is your favourite colour blue?

Chapter One

Miss Diamond was probably our favourite teacher at The Verity Lang Academy and not just because she's a big fan of our band, Lucky Six, either. OK, so she drives us around to our gigs and is totally great when it comes to giving us advice about the entertainment industry, but she's also really careful not to play favourites. She is the singing teacher and vocal coach at the academy and a total inspiration to us students. She's young, too, which means she knows what we're talking about when it comes to music – unlike some of the older members of staff and, dare I say it, our parents! And she's pretty cool too with loads of curly caramel-coloured hair and blue eyes. We always love the trendy clothes she wears. Trust me, she is the *last* teacher we would want to upset. But one morning, during a vocal training lesson, we managed to do just that.

So, there we were in class, with Miss Diamond playing a tune for us all to sing along to and it should've been easy enough but, unfortunately for us, the piano was so ancient the song was completely unrecognisable.

Now, Elle and me normally take Miss Diamond's lessons very seriously and we know how important practice is but today . . . well, we just couldn't concentrate because of the strange piano music. It was just so funny! And you know what it's like when you get the giggles? You just can't stop, and Elle and I kept catching each other's eye. Every time I opened my mouth to sing Elle pulled a silly face and every time *she* opened her mouth *I'd* do the same. I really don't know what got into us.

Each time a duff note rang out, we'd giggle and it didn't take Miss Diamond long to notice what was going on. She stopped playing immediately, a look of surprise on her face at our bad behaviour.

'Lauren!' she shouted, glaring at me and using my full name – which she never normally does. 'And Elle. I'm surprised at you – really I am.'

We both went bright red.

'You're completely disrupting the class.'

I thought that was totally unfair because I knew that everyone had found it really funny – and they'd probably been giggling too – but just hadn't been caught. Annoying, huh? But I thought better not make a scene about it.

'Sorry, Miss Diamond,' I said instead, looking at the floor, aware that all eyes were on me from around the piano.

'What were you both laughing about anyway?'

I looked up at her. 'It's the piano, Miss Diamond,' I said. 'It sounds terrible! You must've noticed. It's so old. It really needs replacing.'

Miss Diamond looked at me a second longer. Then, 'Elle?' she asked, and Elle nodded in agreement. 'Well,' she continued, 'that's as may be but your horseplay is costing everyone else valuable vocal-training time. You give me no option but to

give you a half-hour detention after lessons today to
reflect on your behaviour.'

'Yes, miss,' I said quietly with a sigh.

'Yes, miss,' Elle said.

'In the meantime, I think an apology to the rest
of the class would be a start,' Miss Diamond said.

'Sorry,' I said, in a low sort of a mumble.

'Sorry,' Elle echoed.

The lesson continued and Miss Diamond did her
best with the ropey old piano. Elle and I sang along

with the rest of the class and I had to admit that the awful-sounding tunes just weren't that funny any more.

Later that day, after lessons, Elle and I arrived for our detention.

'What a total drag,' I said.

'I can't believe I've got a detention,' Elle said, pushing a strand of her perfect glossy brown bob behind her ear. 'I've never been to detention in my life!'

'Oh, Miss Perfect!' I said, secretly thinking it funny that our very own band manager and 'Miss Organisation' had landed herself in trouble. 'It wasn't *my* fault so don't blame it all on me.'

'I'm *not* blaming it on you,' she said.

'Yeah, sounds like it.'

'I'm not, Laurie, *really*.'

'You were giggling just as much as I was.'

'I know,' she said. 'That piano sounded so funny.'

I nodded and couldn't help grinning at the memory of it. 'It's really terrible, though,' I said. 'We shouldn't be laughing about it. It should be replaced – and soon. Before it collapses or makes us all sing out of tune.'

We started giggling again.

'It was making me sing all wrong,' I said.

'Me, too,' Elle said. 'As if I had a toad in my throat.'

'A *frog*!' I said. Elle – who's French – is always getting little things like this wrong.

We laughed again – until we saw that Miss Diamond had pulled out two tables and chairs for us to sit at from the pile stacked at the back of the room. And she'd set them a good distance apart so there was no chance of us getting distracted and chatting instead of sitting there in silent boredom.

'Come along now, girls,' she said, nodding to the chairs.

'Well, I guess I'll see you later,' I whispered to Elle as I chose the table and chair to the left of the classroom.

Elle groaned quietly. 'I swear I'll never giggle *ever* again.'

I smiled hopelessly and we took our seats on opposite sides of the room.

Have you ever noticed how time can play tricks on you? When you're having a good time – like when we're rehearsing with our band and everything's going really well – the time will rush by and, before you know it, it's time to go to a boring old maths class. But then, when you're struggling over some terrible page of equations and really have no idea if x equals two, three or five hundred and twenty, time just crawls along. Well, sitting there in the silent classroom was one of the instances when time wasn't in a hurry, which was a real nightmare for me because I'm such a fidget. I just hate being still. It's not natural. I like to be doing something – *always*. So, there I was, sitting like a dope, crossing and uncrossing my legs, examining my fingernails, twisting my hair and making tiny circles with my fingertips on the desk but *still* the time didn't seem to be passing.

I guess we must have been about halfway through our boring old detention when there was a knock on the door and Ms Lang, our headmistress, popped her head round. Ms Lang, in her sixties now, was once a world-famous ballet dancer and I felt totally bad about her seeing me in detention.

'Lauren?' she said, spotting me first. I smiled and nodded towards my fellow sufferer. *'Elle?'* she said, even more surprised to see her there. 'What are you both doing in here so late?'

'Detention, miss,' I explained.

'You two?' she said, obviously shocked that we should be in trouble.

We watched as Ms Lang's little white poodle, Mister Binks, nudged the door open, tail wagging, and headed towards us. He's a bit of a star at the academy. Most people love him and he loves most people. Apart from one of our teachers, Mr Walsh, who – for some reason known only to Mister Binks – he snaps at whenever he gets the opportunity.

I reached down to give him a fuss, his curly coat warm and comforting.

'Hello, Mister Binks,' I said, and he looked up at me with his big dark eyes, obviously enjoying the attention.

'Ah, Miss Diamond,' Ms Lang said, as she noticed her. 'I must say, I'm very surprised to find these two in here.'

'Yes, Ms Lang,' Miss Diamond said with a sigh, which made me feel guilty all over again. 'So am I, but I didn't have a choice, I'm afraid.'

'Really?' Ms Lang looked curious and disappointed all at once.

'Yes, they both had a fit of the giggles during their vocal-training lesson this morning and completely disrupted the class,' Miss Diamond said.

'Oh, dear,' Ms Lang said. 'And what caused that, may I ask?'

Miss Diamond cleared her throat and looked a little embarrassed, as if she were afraid of telling the truth. 'The piano.'

'The piano?'

'Yes, Ms Lang. Mr Walsh has had a look at it for me but he says it's beyond tuning. It really has seen better days, unfortunately.'

'I see,' Ms Lang said with a strange sort of smile. For a moment, I imagined Ms Lang as a teenage girl, totally sure that she too would have been giggling uncontrollably at the sound the piano had made that morning. 'Well,' she continued, 'I'm sure you'll all be rather pleased with my news, then.'

I looked across the room towards Elle and she shrugged.

'One of my dear old friends,' Ms Lang said, and, as she said the word *friends*, I couldn't help

148

noticing that her face lit up, 'Monsieur Philippe Montpelier, the French pianist, has left his fabulous piano to me in his will.'

Miss Diamond's eyes widened at the news and I exchanged glances with Elle again.

'And I would be very happy to donate it to the vocal training classroom,' Ms Lang concluded, with a broad smile. 'It will look wonderfully at home here, I'm sure, and I know you will take very good care of it.'

'Oh, Ms Lang!' Miss Diamond said, getting up from her chair. 'This will solve all our problems. It's very generous of you. And you can be sure that we will cherish it.'

Ms Lang waved a hand dismissively in the air as if her gift were nothing really – like she gave pianos away every day of the week.

Elle and I got up from our seats too in the excitement, completely forgetting that we were still in detention.

'Isn't that great news, girls?' Miss Diamond said.

'Brilliant!' I said, nodding enthusiastically.

'Yes, thanks, Ms Lang!' Elle said.

'Just think,' I giggled, 'no more duff notes.'

'No more appalling scales,' Elle laughed.

'And no more inappropriate fits of giggles,' Miss Diamond said, trying to hide a smirk.

Elle and I nodded. It was really cool. We couldn't wait for that new piano to arrive.

Collect all the titles in the series